HEALED BY THE FIRE

ARTEMIS LUPINE SERIES, BOOK THREE

CATHERINE BANKS

Mom and Dad, thank you for your endless support. You mean the world to me and your support means even more!

Lea, thank you for your PA-ing help and beta assistance on this series. You are a wonderful person and a great friend.

Special thanks to the following people
who backed my Kickstarter and helped
t these gorgeous books out into the world.

Amanda Jenkins
Anij Fallows
Arlene Medder
Brandy Robinson
Ceciley Snook
D. T. Brook
Davide B.
Deissy Hermunslie
Emily Suzanne Davis
Emjrabbitwolf
Fawn of the Woods
Francesco Tehrani
Gary Phillips
Helen Jensen
Jamie Forster
Jeff Lewis
nnifer & Jamie Wallace
Jennifer Laslie
Jon Tarbox
Ken Anderson
Kylie Corley

Louise Kendall
Matthea W. Ross
MelX
Michelle Fritz
Michelle Johnson
Michelle R. McFarlin
R.J. Blain
Ran Frimark
Russell Nohelty
Russell Ventimeglia
Stormie Harlan
Synergica
Taka Angevine
Tara Harrington
Zack Newcomb
Amanda Haynes
Erin Hayes
Amber
Emma
The Creative Fund
Rebecca Laffar-Smith

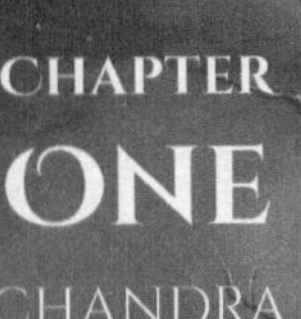

CHAPTER

ONE

CHANDRA

The sun was just cresting the mountains as I walked down the concrete sidewalk towards Preternatural Potions, the best magic shop within one hundred miles of the coven where I lived. I admired the buildings around me that still looked freshly painted even after thirty years, and I wondered which spell was used to protect the paint from dirt and sun bleaching.

I didn't remember what the human world looked like before the uprising, but from the pictures I'd seen I agreed with Selene that the preternaturally run world was definitely better looking. The leaders, however, were not better for the world. Now we not only had monarchs heading each of the races, but we also had a dictator who was worse than any human politician could have been.

A tall, light-skinned, red-haired dhampir stepped out of the store in front of me. I forced myself to lower my eyes respectfully and move out of his way instead of reacting as I desired. If only I remembered who I was, what my name was

1

at the very least, it would help me understand more about my reactions.

"Good morning, miss," the dhampir said kindly.

"Morning, sir," I replied as I continued past him.

I snuck a glance back, but thankfully he was still rooted in the spot, following me only with his eyes. Only a few more blocks and then I'd be safely at my destination.

The sun rose and the true beauty of the town was revealed. Every vampire noble was given executive rights to decide what their territories would look like, except for specific restrictions that the Vampire King, the dictator of the world, gave. The buildings were constructed from wood and painted in what looked like a light blue color at night, but when the morning light hit the buildings it revealed its gorgeous bicolor. The paint was actually a dual tone of blue and purple, which changed continuously depending upon the way you looked at it.

"Owner?" asked a short, burly goblin at the crosswalk in front of me.

The goblins had been in the deserts of the Middle East and Northern Africa during the human reign. I wasn't sure if their resilience had come from living in the deserts for thousands of years or if their resilience had allowed them to adapt to living in the deserts, but the fact remained that they were a preserving and strong race which could adapt to any climate quickly. Once the preternaturals had taken over, the goblins spread out from the deserts to the more temperate climates around the world, mainly living in the Northern Hemisphere.

"Selene, leader of the Western Coven of Witches," I answered automatically.

The goblin, an enforcer for the vampires, nodded and waved me across the street.

How nice of you to let me pass. I continued on my way. Little did the goblin know that I could toast him out of his boots faster than he could yell for his mother. I was glad that he hadn't asked to see my brand since the one I had tattooed on the back of my neck wasn't the witch's. I actually didn't know whose it was.

I finally arrived at the store and pushed the door open. The scent of jasmine flooded my nose and the sounds of a rainforest inundated my ears. For a moment, I was teleported to a tropical forest where animals much different than the ones I was familiar with ruled and where humanity hadn't been able to overwhelm. The door closed behind, me and the spell broke slightly, allowing me to regain my senses while still being able to relax. It was one of the best spells I had ever encountered, and it did its job of allowing shoppers to browse stress-free.

The large store seemed small due to the wall to wall, floor to ceiling shelves. Various sized glass vials, bags, boxes and cages which held everything from toad tongues to herbs to test rats lined the shelves. Each had elegantly written labels hanging from them with product descriptions and prices. In the center of the store was a large circular wooden table which had sale items as well as the most commonly purchased potions, charms, crystals and other magical artifacts. I knew this was only a sampling of what Preternatural Potions offered and you only had to ask the clerk to run to the back for other items.

I looked towards the front counter, which was nothing more than a white elm trunk shaved into a rectangular shape. Not surprisingly, there was no one behind the counter. The clerk, Dionysus, had a drinking problem and was either drunk, crabby because he needed a drink, or passed out in the back of the store. I was actually pleased that he wasn't there to pester me. He was constantly toying with me and hiding ingredients that I required on a weekly basis so that I had to ask him, and ask him politely, for them.

One of the witches in my coven told me that he had interfered with something the Queen of the Sidhe had been planning for months because he had been intoxicated, so they sent him to operate the store. He hated every moment of it, especially since the vampires refused to let him decorate the interior in a more pleasing, non-sterile manner.

I walked to the first shelf and grabbed three vials of ingredients I needed. I should have grabbed a basket from the stack sitting beside the door, but I moved on to the next shelf instead, grabbing another vial and cradling them all in my arms.

"Hello," said a voice like bottled sunshine.

I jumped in surprise and caught three of the four vials I'd had in my arms. I could have grabbed the fourth, but I was supposed to be playing human so I couldn't use my preternatural speed. I waited for the sound of shattering glass, but was greeted with only soft laughter.

I turned around and made my way past leg muscles straining against jeans, to an incredibly muscled stomach and torso to a smile that stole my breath and to eyes that made my knees wobble. To say that the man standing in front of me was handsome was like calling the ocean a puddle. His blue eyes sparkled like a clear summer's day. I dropped to my knees and bowed until my forehead touched the ground.

"I'm s-s-sorry, s-sir," I stuttered fearfully. "I didn't m-m-mean to l-look upon your f-face." I hated it when I stuttered, but it was a side effect from having been in wolf form for over ten years straight. Selene, the leader of the witch coven I lived with, had found me and helped recuperate me back into a human, or at least as much of one as I could be considering I was half Sidhe and half werewolf.

He sighed. "Broken. How can you be so broken?" My wolf snarled softly and as I feared he'd heard. "Did you just snarl?"

I swallowed. "N-n-no Sir." Words were still hard to say at times for me, especially when I was nervous.

He scoffed. "Stand up, Chandra. I'm not going to punish you. As if that would work anyways. Are you here to shop or browse?"

I stood up slowly and whispered, "Shop."

"How could this have happened? Doesn't even recognize me!" I kept still since he was obviously talking to himself and I had no clue what he was talking about.

My body trembled softly as I stood near him. He was the most dominant male wolf I'd ever met, and he was calling to every fiber of my wolf side. The urge to rub my face against his was almost overpowering for a moment as I fought with my animal urges. I knew he wouldn't be able to sense my wolf since Selene had given me a necklace with a charm which concealed my true genetics, one so powerful, no one except the most dominant of each race could break it, but I was worried. If he guessed for one second that I was a halfbreed, he would take me captive. I'd heard awful stories of halfbreeds seized from their home, their work, or even from the arms of their lover to be taken away and never seen or heard from again.

"Is this all or are there more items you need to shop for?" he asked, taking a step closer to me.

I stepped back from him and bumped into the shelves. "I have m-more."

"Very well. Finish shopping."

I waited until I heard and felt him walk away before looking up at the shelves again. I'd never *felt* somebody like I felt him. It was as if we were connected somehow. I shook my head and dismissed the ridiculous notion. I looked back up at the top shelf where Dionysus had placed my ingredient. I couldn't jump up and get it. I looked toward the register where the alpha watched me.

Why was one of the most powerful alphas working in a magic shop? Why did I feel so strongly towards him when I'd never met him before? How did he know my name?

"S-sir?"

He lifted a brow. "Yes?"

I pointed up. "I n-n-need that item. The usual clerk likes to t-toy with me by placing them out of reach. Could you perhaps…retrieve it for me?" The longer I talked with him, the less I stuttered and the surer of myself I felt.

He walked around the counter and towards me. I felt my heartbeat pick up as I watched his graceful movements, his feet light on the floor, barely making a sound as he stalked towards me. I forced myself to remain still as he walked up to me and stopped inches away. "Which item?" he asked softly. I inhaled the smell of him and closed my eyes as a memory of lying against him and inhaling his scent played across my closed eyelids. *A memory or a fantasy?* I wasn't sure.

I shook my body and cleared my throat before saying, "The bottle on the top shelf." I took two steps back to give him room and watched as he jumped up and grabbed the bottle easily.

He held the bottle out to me. "Anything else?"

You. No, you in wolf form, running with me in my wolf form. I bit my lip as I stopped the whine trying to escape. I'd been a lone wolf since Selene found me and being this close to a male wolf hurt. I wanted a pack mate. I wanted a wolf to run with me.

I bit my lip harder, drawing blood into my mouth, which helped clear my head. "I just have a few more things to pick up." I turned away from him and quickly grabbed the six other items I needed and set them on the counter in front of him.

He put the items in bags and set the bags on the counter. Since every preternatural group had slaves that contributed to the world, we no longer used currency. Basically, since everyone contributed, no one owed each other money. It was the vampire's ideal society, utopian socialism where they weren't the ones who had to contribute, only their slaves did.

I reached out for the bags, but instead of pushing them towards me, he carried them to the door and pushed the door open for me. Warm air blew into the store and his scent into my face. I inhaled and rememorized his scent. *Rememorized? When had I memorized it before?*

"Are you feeling alright?" he asked softly.

"Y-y-yes. Thank you." I took the bags from him, being extra careful not to touch him.

"Broken. I don't understand how she can be so *broken*?" he said angrily as he gripped his black hair.

I should have been afraid, but instead I turned around and demanded, "Why do you keep calling me *broken*?"

His face went completely blank, becoming the type of mask people wear when hiding their true emotions. "I did not mean to offend you."

I scoffed and rolled my eyes at him. "Right, because calling me *broken* shouldn't offend me. I know you're a bigwig in the werewolf community, but just because you're powerful doesn't mean you can go around calling people *broken*, especially when you have no idea what kind of crap they've been through!" I was yelling by the end of my tirade and my face was red with anger.

He smiled and bowed at the waist. "My apologies."

I thought I'd seen it all, but I never would have imagined that the Prince of the Werewolves would be bowing and apologizing to me. He straightened, and in doing so, spied the charm sitting at the base of my throat. Before I could react, he grabbed it and growled. I gasped as his eyes changed to golden wolf's eyes and a blanket of some invisible force surrounded my body. I'd felt power being used on me before, but it had never been so much and as strong as his. I couldn't move. I couldn't breathe. I was dying and he wasn't even touching me.

Spots began to cover my vision as he fought to break the spell Selene had placed on the charm, and his power continued to suffocate me. A spark of lightning burst from the charm to his hand, making him yell out in pain and drop the charm. His power disappeared, and I was able to breathe once again. I fell to the ground on my hands and knees, gasping and coughing for breath.

"Selene," he growled softly.

I looked up at him and could suddenly see the ghost outline of his wolf's face around his human face. Only were-wolves could see the image, when a fellow wolf was close to changing. Against all warnings in my brain, I stood up, reached out, and touched the muzzle of the ghost wolf. "Black. You're a black wolf."

He spoke so softly I barely heard him, even with my enhanced werewolf hearing, "Yes."

I ran my hand along the ears of the ghost wolf and swore I saw him shiver. "I...I've had dreams about a black wolf, but I was told there was only one pure black wolf in existence."

His wolf side was close to taking over, and his words were short and clipped as though he was having trouble forming them, "Only one black wolf. Only me."

"Are there any white wolves?" I asked. I knew I shouldn't be asking him, but I had to know.

"Only one," he said. I looked up into his eyes and saw the smile I thought I'd heard in his voice. "Only you."

Before I could jump back, he grabbed my wrist. I gasped as he covered me in his power again. It felt like I was drowning in a sea of fire, making it impossible for me to breathe. The spell Selene had placed around me broke, the talisman around my neck shattered, and the world went black.

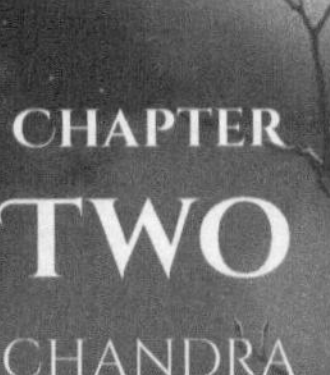

CHAPTER
TWO

CHANDRA

I woke up slowly and realized I was in my wolf form. I opened my eyes and found myself looking into another pair of amber wolf eyes. I scurried back away from him, and he whined softly. *It's alright. I won't harm you.*

My wolf whimpered and took control from me, running forward and rubbing our head against his chest. He licked my face gently and whined happily.

I regained control and pulled away. It had been years since I'd had problems with control of my wolf side. I wrestled with my wolf for one full minute until I finally regained control and changed to human form. I gasped from the quick changes and curled into a ball as the sharp tingling pains wore off.

His fur rippled like water and then he crouched before me as a man. "Are you alright?"

I backed away from him, covering my body as well as I could. "What did you do?" The desire to touch him was burning my fingertips. My lips burned with a memory of kissing his. "How do I know you?"

He held his hand out to me, and I backed away until my

back hit the wall. He dropped his hand and I could see the pain in his eyes.

"There is much to tell you. You and I are mates…"

I stared at him in utter disbelief, but my wolf side acknowledged him as our mate. How could he be my mate if I had never met him before? I shook my head. "No. You can't be my mate." I picked up my shredded pants and shirt and ran around him. He called after me, but I ignored his calls. I stumbled into my clothes as I ran out the door and then yelled as loud as I could, "Draco-blu!"

I heard the flapping of large wings and then the generated wind pressed down on me, flattening me to the ground. The alpha crouched down, walking slowly towards me, but I knew he wouldn't make it to me before Draco-Blu did.

Draco-Blu descended and I admired his beauty as he landed over me. He was the largest dragon I'd ever seen; the top of my head barely touched his underbelly. His build reminded me of a horse, four large, muscular legs which carried a sleek, but powerful body. Draco was the title given to the king of the dragons. Blu is the only blue dragon to be given the title in the history of the dragons. I asked him if there was a difference in power by their colors, but he simply answered that blue dragons were very rare. He was one of my friends and I had the special privilege of simply calling him Blu. His blue scales shimmered in the sun and the white talons resting on either side of me reflected my face.

"Oh, shit," said the alpha werewolf who had stopped advancing and now stood in front of Blu.

Blu roared, but the alpha held his ground. "Ares of the Werewolves! I challenge you…"

"Sorry, Draco, but I cannot accept. Chandra, we will see

each other again. Soon," the alpha said before turning and disappearing around the corner of a nearby building.

Blu snorted a puff of smoke. "Well, that was interesting. Are you alright, Hatchling?"

I shuddered as I stood up. I grabbed onto his head and he lifted it up, setting me down just in front of his shoulders, at the base of his neck. "I don't know, Blu. I don't know what happened. I think I might know him from before. He...he knew I was part wolf. He said we were mates."

"You need to speak to Selene, and we need to visit the Council," he said. I swallowed nervously at the thought of visiting the dragon council. They were powerful and would know how to help me, but they scared me more than a horde of vampires overcome by bloodlust. I gripped Draco's scales, which were textured enough for me to hang onto yet not overly rough and painful after long rides.

He flapped his wings and zoomed up into the sky. I wished I could spread my wings and fly beside him instead of on his back, but if I did that and a vampire or a vampire ally saw me, they would try to capture me or just kill me. Mixed bloods were not welcome in the New Preternatural World.

"It's a good thing that I escorted you today and stayed just on the outskirts of the town while you shopped," said Blu as he glided across the winds.

I sighed sadly. "Yes, I suppose it is, although I do not like having to be protected to go out." I lifted my arms out to my sides, enjoying the feel of the wind on my body.

The concrete jungle that had once been the human world was gone, destroyed by the preternaturals to allow a more organic landscape to emerge.

We flew over various small towns and villages, children waving to Blu excitedly while the adults cowered in the doorways. Blu's massive shadow covered two buildings at once, scaring a coop full of chickens and a stable of horses at the same time.

"Are there any other errands you need to run or are we heading straight back to the coven?" he asked as he tilted sideways, making a large circle over a crystal blue lake below.

I looked longingly at the lake, wishing to go for a swim. I knew I should head straight back to the coven to report to Selene, but I was shaky and needed to do something relaxing. "I guess we could stop for a short swim," I said finally.

Blu roared happily and dove straight down towards the lake, folding his wings in tight against his body. As he plummeted, I wrapped my arms around his neck so I wouldn't separate from him. The impact from slamming into the water almost dislodged me from Blu's back, but I managed to hang on. I fought the urge to gasp at the shock of the cold water surrounding me and released my hold, kicking my legs quickly to the surface. Blu spun around under the water, heading back towards me and shoved his nose under my feet, pushing me up and through the surface of the water. I flew up into the air thirty feet and then dove back down, barely making a splash as I reentered the water.

Blu swam in lazy circles, slicing through it with his tail. I splashed Blu's nose with a small wave of water, inviting play. Blu skimmed his tail across the water, sending a wave to cover me, which sent me back down below the surface.

Blu laughed hysterically, shooting fire from his nose in his delight. He was one of my best friends because he could go from being the fierce leader of the dragons to the silliest being on the planet and playing childish games with me.

We played until the sun stood in the center of the sky and both Blu and my stomachs growled loudly.

As we flew in the air towards the coven, I closed my eyes and enjoyed the warmth of the sun drying me. "Thank you," I whispered. He seemed to always know what I needed.

He hummed happily. "You are welcome, Hatchling. Now, let's get you home."

We flew the last ten miles in silence, enjoying the other's quiet, but pleasurable company and the moment of contentment. The coven came into view, and I admired my home.

The coven was a large fortress with thirty foot walls surrounding the one thousand acres property. The walls were really only there to keep out the local wildlife and for the perimeter spell, which alerted Selene to intruders. The main building was fifty feet high and had several hundred rooms, not including the kitchen and common areas. There were three smaller buildings, the larger of which was used for teaching the younger witches. The building to the left of that was the lab which was used for experimenting with new spells. The third building was a mystery to me. Selene had told me only that it was used for the witches' committee hearings. There was also a small stable area where we bred cows for Blu and the other dragons who visited to eat.

Two gardens took up three acres total on either side of the main building and a forest of twenty acres stood in the back corner of their property. The witches hardly ever used the forest, but I used it frequently.

Blu dropped down into the courtyard of the coven and roared a welcoming to the witches. Several witches were outside and they bowed respectfully to him. A teenage witch walked to the stable area to catch one of the cows for him. I slipped down his side and leg and smiled at the witches who were outside. I turned to Blu and bowed. "Thank you, Blu."

He flicked his forked tongue out across my cheek. "You are

welcome, Hatchling. I will return with a summons once I've spoken to the Council. I will have Fira visit you in my absence."

Blu gulped down the cow the teenager brought out and then burped a stream of flame into the air happily.

He dropped his head down and I hugged his nose, laying a kiss on the tip of it. "Be safe and may the wind speed your flight."

He lifted one of his large front claws and brushed a scale off to land on the ground. "Take this. You may need the magic stored within it."

I picked up the scale and felt the power radiating from it. "This is a very precious gift. I will cherish it."

He rubbed his nose gently against my body once and then took to the sky. He roared a goodbye and then disappeared from my sight. I clutched the scale to my chest and raced to my room as the pain I'd been hiding intensified.

My heart hurt and the physical pain of the absence of the alpha was like a hot iron stabbing me in the stomach. I dashed inside the main building and up the three flights of stairs to my room in the west wing. Thankfully, I made it to my room unnoticed and unquestioned. I softly shut my bedroom door and sighed in relief.

"Who broke my spell?" Selene asked from behind me.

I growled and spun around, ready to attack. It took a moment for me to realize it was Selene and calm myself. "Sorry. Sorry," I apologized as I lowered my eyes and stepped back from her.

Selene was average height and build for a woman, but the incredible amount of power she possessed made her seem bigger and more intimidating. She had black hair that looked like it was streaked with blue in the sun and the deepest brown eyes I had ever seen.

She stood up from my bed where she had been sitting and placed her hand on my face. I closed my eyes as she closed hers and then she chanted magic words, which weaved a spell to replay the day's events in our heads for her to see.

Selene removed her hand and gasped as the last image of Blu diving into the lake finished. "No. No it cannot be true," she said in disbelief as she stepped back from me.

I fell onto my bed, tired from the changes and the magic which had been used against me. "What is it? Who is he to me? Is he really my mate?"

She shook her head, refusing to answer and then hurried from my room, closing the door behind her. The pain was intensifying so I closed my eyes and let myself sleep in an effort to try to heal myself.

"CHANDRA. Chandra, wake up! You're going to miss story time!" a young female yelled at me from beside the bed.

I opened one eye and looked at the seven-year-old girl standing with her hands on her hips beside me. She was small for her age, but what she lacked in height she made up for in attitude.

Once I had been rehabilitated, Selene decided that helping children find their powers would help calm the anger and despair that she insisted surrounded me. So, I taught the younger witches and the young girl in front of me, Juliana, was one of my favorite students.

I showered and dressed quickly so as not to keep the impatient child waiting too long. When done, Juliana grabbed my hand and dragged me down the stairs to one of the common rooms already filled with witches. This room was carpeted with soft blue shag ideal for lounging on. Many of the older witches smiled and bowed respectfully to me. I returned the salute and then sat down among the young children who crowded closer as I situated myself on the floor.

It'd been a long time since I'd come out of my room without my talisman on and many of the children ran their fingertips along the designs on my arms. I relaxed as their touch soothed the pack animal within me, but another part of me felt like a wire pulled taut. Somehow, I knew that this feeling wouldn't subside until I was near the werewolf prince again.

Selene stepped out in front of the room and the crowd instantly hushed their chatter. She sat in her chair with her head in her hands. "We will not be having story time tonight," she said softly. The children groaned and the adults looked at each other nervously. Selene began talking again and everyone silenced to hear her. "I am calling an emergency council of *all* fully realized witches to begin immediately. Jessica will be in charge of the teens and the children. Jessica, please take them to their rooms now. Everyone else please pick up a chair and form a semi-circle facing me."

I reassured the children and then grabbed a chair from the stack in the back. I started to set my chair beside one of the other witches, but Selene looked up at me and ordered, "Sit in the center, Chandra."

I swallowed the fear I felt and set my chair in the center. I waited until all of the other witches were seated before taking mine. I could feel the nervous energy around me and heard it in the shifting of chairs and the quickened breath of the witches.

"I have seen something which I need verified. I have seen something which may tell Chandra her true identity. The problem we are facing is Chandra herself."

I stared at Selene in shock. "Me? I'm a problem?"

Selene smiled. "Your powers are the problem. I think, as a group, we may be able to help you suppress your powers long enough to find your true self, but I am not certain."

"What about the dragons?" asked Angelina, one of the witches of whom I was most fond.

Every eye turned to me and I forced myself not to fidget. "Draco-Blu left earlier to speak to the dragon council and see if they would allow me an audience."

Selene tapped her chin with one long finger. "I'd like to hear all of your thoughts. My fear is that if we try and fail, we may permanently injure Chandra or ourselves. However, the dragons are a much older and much more powerful race and may be able to do it."

"Do you have her real name?" asked Silvia.

Selene avoided looking at me and simply nodded. "I have her first name."

I stared at her in utter disbelief. "You know my first name? My true first name?!" I asked, glaring at her.

She looked at me and licked her lips nervously. "Yes. I have not revealed it to you for fear of harming you. If you learned your true first name, but could not uncover the rest of your name on your own, it could destroy you."

"That's ridiculous!" I yelled, my hands forming fists.

"She's right," said the softest spoken witch in the coven, Mauve. "If you hear your first name and accept it as true, but cannot uncover the rest of it, the memories of your past could overwhelm you and cause you to go into a coma."

Every witch looked down at their hands in silence. I'd

heard about the story of Mauve's sister, but hadn't believed it was true. Until now.

I looked at Selene. "What about the prince? Can't he help me?"

Selene sighed. "I do not know whether the prince is who he says he is or not and even if he is, I have no way of knowing if he is strong enough to assist you."

"So, either I have the prince and the coven help or the dragons?"

Selene shook her head. "The dragons will need the prince to help them as well. So, either the coven or the dragons will help you and the prince."

"Which prince?" asked Silvia.

"The werewolf one," I said quietly. "I forget his name."

Silvia opened her mouth and Selene placed a silencing spell on her before Silvia had uttered the first syllable. "No one is to reveal his name!" The room quaked with Selene's command and all of the gathered witches bowed in submission.

I stood up against her power and glared at her. "This is ridiculous! I want to know who I am and who he is! I've been alone for too long! I can't stand it anymore, Selene!"

"You won't have to," said a quiet male voice.

I'd never seen so many witches use the same spell so quickly. Before I'd even turned toward the voice, the speaker was off the ground and imprisoned in an invisible grip in the air. He was handsome, looked to be in his early twenties with black skin and white patterns down his arms. I could guess what he was instantly, but held my tongue until I knew for sure.

Selene walked towards the intruder slowly, her skin

sparkling with magic. "Who are you and how did you get into my coven unnoticed?"

The intruder smiled. "I am a friend of those who have been looking for the woman you are protecting. I have come to offer her solace from the pain of loneliness that she has been enduring, until such a time as she can be reunited with her rightful pack."

Selene nodded and all of the witches released their spells and allowed the man to drop to the ground. He landed on his feet as though they'd dropped him one foot instead of twelve. "Come, we shall speak in my office," Selene said softly.

The man bowed his head respectfully and then walked slowly towards me. I inhaled, and my body quivered in excitement. He stopped in front of me, towering over me at more than six feet tall, and inhaled loudly. "What do they call you?" he asked.

I smiled up at him and inhaled again. "Chandra."

He looked into my eyes and asked, "Are you alright, Chandra?"

I kept eye contact, refusing to accept him as dominant over me. "I am better with your presence. What is your name?"

He dropped eye contact and recognized me as dominant. "My name is Theseus. I will return as soon as I am done speaking to your coven leader. Can you wait that long for a run?"

The scent of his wolf was stronger the longer he stood by me. I opened my mouth a little wider to catch more of his scent. "Yes, I will prepare myself mentally while you are speaking to Selene."

He smiled happily and followed Selene to her room. I

dropped to my knees on the ground, smiling happily. A half-breed wolf! I'd never thought I'd find another halfbreed wolf.

It was strange that I wasn't interested in him. Why wasn't I? He was attractive, yet I wasn't intrigued by him in any other way than for a pack mate and for our similar lineage.

Silvia dropped down next to me and looked in my eyes. "Are you alright, dear? Did he hurt you?"

I laughed and shook my head. "No." I looked up at all of the concerned faces of the witches around me. "You don't know?"

They all frowned in confusion. Silvia asked, "Don't know what?"

I smiled. Of course, they didn't know they couldn't smell him like I could. "He's a halfbreed wolf like me. He's the same mixture as me."

They all looked at me in shock as what I said absorbed and then they all started asking me questions at once. I raised my hand and silenced them. "I don't want to talk about it. I know what he is because I can smell it and feel it. If you want to know more, ask Selene." I stood up and hurried to my room before they could ask me any other questions.

I was finally going to run with another wolf! I brushed my hair until not a single knot could be found and then sat on the floor to meditate and calm my nerves. He wouldn't appreciate it if I bit his head off when I changed.

Just as I calmed myself enough to relax, someone knocked on my door. "Come in," I said softly.

Selene stepped into the room and closed the door behind her. "What he says is true," she stated simply, "He was sent here to be a companion for you until such a time as we can figure out who you really are. He is waiting out in the garden for you."

Standing up slowly, I watched Selene. She was hiding something. "What else did he say?"

She sighed. "He told me what he knew of your past and if what he says is true, you're in more danger than I originally thought. I hope Draco-Blu comes for you soon."

I followed her out of the room and out of the main building. "You are afraid. For me or the coven?" I asked.

She smiled at me. "Your ability to read me is a testament to the amount of time we have spent together. I am afraid for both. If you are who he says, the vampires will stop at nothing to get you before your true mate does. The vampires are powerful and I'd prefer they not view me as a threat."

"I will stay within our boundaries until Blu returns," I promised as Theseus came into sight.

Selene smiled. "Go on. Enjoy your run and your new friend."

I hugged her once and then changed forms before running to him. He was twice my size and a dark red color. *Are you ready for our run?* He asked through my mind.

I bobbed my muzzle up and down. *Yes, but we must stay within the boundaries of the coven.*

He sneezed. *As if you needed to tell me the dangers out there.*

Before I could ask what he meant, he took off at a full run. I yipped excitedly and chased after him. I pounced on top of him, knocking him to the ground. He rolled and jumped at me, but I dashed out of his reach and then dashed back to nip at his tail. He growled and snapped at me, but I was already ten feet away with my front half down on the ground and my bottom half up in the air. I wagged my tail happily. *You're pretty slow for a halfbreed.*

He lifted his lips in a wolf smile. *I haven't shown you my true speed yet. I've just been letting you enjoy yourself.*

Likewise.

His back paws dug into the ground as he prepared to charge me, and I sprang forward, darting right past him and nipping his flank before circling him and returning to my original spot. In truth, I had no idea how fast other werewolves or halfbreed wolves were since I'd never been around them, but I knew I was fast.

In a blink of an eye he dashed forward and nipped my flank. I spun around, but he was behind me again and nipped my tail. It was time not to hold back anymore. I followed his movements and then leapt up and over him when he tried to nip me again. He slid as he tried to stop and then I smacked into his side, slamming him to the ground and stood over him. *You're fast, but not fast enough.* I darted away and yipped happily. *Catch me if you can!*

For two hours, we ran and played in wolf form, stopping only to drink from a shallow stream which wound its way through the center of the coven's property. I watched the fish swimming through it, going with the flow of the current and wished for a free life to swim where I wanted.

After I had quelled the burning in my throat from our vigorous play I took off running again, but the beat of wings and the pressure of wind alerted me to the presence of a dragon.

"Run, Chandra!" yelled Fira, Blu's son.

I spun around just as Fira gripped Theseus in one of his front red claws. I changed forms in less than a second and shot Fira in the nose with my fire, stopping him just as he was preparing to toast Theseus. Fira dropped Theseus, and I ran forward to catch him, but he changed forms and released his wings just in time to soften his landing.

Fira roared at me. "Why did you do that?!"

"He is a friend, Fira, not an attacker. Besides, my fire does not hurt dragons so stop acting like I've harmed you."

Fira dropped to the ground and shook out his body. "No, your Sidhe fire does not harm us, but it is never pleasant to have unfamiliar fire touch your body."

"I had to stop you from killing him. Thank you for your protection and concern, but Theseus here is a friend."

Fira looked at Theseus a moment and then snorted. "A wolf-Sidhe halfbreed like you, Chandra. How interesting."

Theseus looked from me to the dragon and then back at me. "You know dragons?"

Fira dropped his head and allowed me to pet him. "Yes. I am friends with the dragons. Well, at least Draco-Blu and Fira here are my friends," I answered.

Theseus started towards me, but Fira growled.

"I do not trust him, Chandra," Theseus said.

I stopped petting Fira and looked at Theseus. "I do not care if you trust him or not. Fira is my friend and has been protecting me for the past several years. You will have to learn to accept the dragons or you will have to leave."

Theseus gaped at me. "You would send me away? You would live in solitude again?"

I shuddered and whispered, "I would not like it, but I love the dragons and I will not dishonor their protection of me just for companionship. Besides, you are only coming to me now while they have been protecting me for a decade. Who would you trust more?"

Fira yawned. "I need to return to the nest. Will you be alright for tonight?"

I nodded and placed a kiss on the tip of his nose. "Thank you, my friend."

Fira growled once more at Theseus and then took to the

sky. I watched him, longing to fly with him and then turned to Theseus who was watching me with an intense curiosity. "I am sorry if I offended you," I said softly.

Theseus smiled and then wrapped his arms around me in a hug. "You are loyal, which is a wonderful quality, especially in these dark times."

I relaxed into his hold and inhaled his scent loudly.

"Well, isn't this cute? Two halfbreeds comforting each other," snarled a menacing voice.

I spun around and growled at the vampire standing before me. "How did you get in here?" I cast a Monitum spell, which created a butterfly that flew to Selene to notify her that I was in trouble and quickly moved back from the vampire, pushing Theseus backwards with me.

"I have my ways, female. So, you found her at last, did you Theseus?"

Theseus growled. "You know that I have to kill you now, right? I can't let you report back to Maurice."

The name Maurice sounded familiar and a headache began in the front of my skull. I rubbed at it and took a step back, hiding slightly behind Theseus instead of standing protectively in front of him as I had been.

I felt Selene's presence growing closer and hoped she would be there in time.

"Has she found herself yet?" the vampire asked.

"It seems we are all full of discoveries tonight. One of which is that I have a break in my barrier," said Selene as she finally arrived. The vampire hissed at Selene, but she only laughed and said, "Oh, you poor stupid vampire. Did you really think you could come into my coven and threaten one of my sisters? I think your kind has grown cocky." She raised her hands and then sunlight covered the vampire. He screamed once and then disintegrated into ash.

Theseus gasped and stared at the pile of ash. "I've never seen that spell before."

Selene smiled and put her arm around my shoulders. "Chandra discovered it." She looked at my pinched face and her smile disappeared. "What is it? What's wrong?"

"My head hurts," I said softly.

Selene looked at Theseus. "You swore you wouldn't reveal anyone's name!"

He swallowed. "I did not mean to. It was a name I thought she would have heard already."

Selene looked at him. "Who?"

"The vampire king," he said softly.

"Maurice," I whispered and then screamed in pain as my head throbbed and an image of a large winery in some foreign place and a handsome man whose smile was pure evil clouded my vision. "Why does it hurt when I say his name?"

Selene placed her hands on my head and started chanting. Theseus picked my hand up in his and then placed his wrist under my nose to distract my senses. Ten minutes later the pain was finally gone. Selene glared at Theseus. "You will remember next time. We cannot afford to lose her nor have her powers released."

Theseus bowed. "I apologize. I will remember."

Selene walked briskly away without looking back. I started to stand, but Theseus picked me up instead. I looked at his face and frowned. "You look familiar, like I've met you before."

He shook his head. "That's not possible."

"Maybe I know a relative of yours then?"

Theseus shrugged. "Perhaps."

I waited for him to tell me more, but he just walked in silence as he carried me back towards the main building. "Who are your parents?" I finally asked.

He sighed. "Chandra, I cannot say any names. You only heard one name of a person you aren't even tied to and it caused you pain. What do you think hearing a name of a person you are tied to will do?"

"You know my true name, don't you?"

Theseus sighed. "I hope Draco-Blu comes back soon. You ask too many questions which could kill you or everyone else."

I rolled my eyes. "And you are a dramatist."

THREE

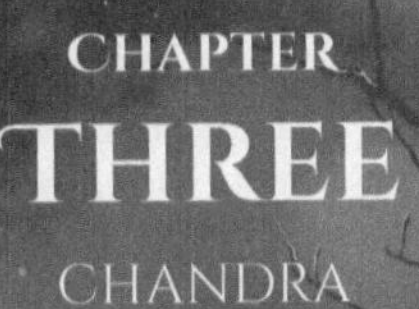

Trying to work with the children was impossible with Theseus around. For one, they couldn't take their eyes off of him. The girls were mesmerized by his beauty while the boys were mesmerized by his masculinity. Second, my classroom had been transformed from a children's introduction to magic class to a coven's introduction to halfbreeds class.

Did it bother me that they wanted to learn more now that Theseus was here? Yes. Why wasn't I interesting enough for them to analyze? Or was it because I didn't know my past or how I'd learned my powers, while Theseus did?

Theseus stood at the front of the room shirtless with his back to us, his body shining as he called his power and released his wings. Those who were gathered watched intently as he pulled his wings out and put them back again and again.

"Does it hurt?" one of the girls asked.

He shook his head. "No, it feels good actually. Like when you have a spot in your back that needs to pop and then you turn just the right way and it pops."

"Unless someone forces your wings out. That hurts," I said quietly as I remembered the painful event.

He turned and looked at me in shock. "Who did that to you?"

"A full blooded Sidhe who likes to annoy me," I answered vaguely. I was not about to tell him it was Dionysus. As much as he annoyed me, he had kept my true lineage a secret.

"Can you show us the process of shifting to warrior form?" James, the smallest but most intelligent boy in my class, asked.

What would the werewolf prince's half shift look like?

Theseus closed his eyes, and his glow faded. I pushed myself off of the wall I had been leaning on and walked out of the classroom. Obviously, my services were not needed here.

I walked north and entered the arched hedge which led into the rose garden and the mini labyrinth Selene had created. The witches had a spell on the garden which kept the flowers constantly blooming. Once I entered it, no other scent except roses filled my nose. Bees hummed as they pollinated the roses and went about their business. The bees never bothered us, even when we entered the labyrinth, so we never bothered them.

I made my way through the small labyrinth, running my hands along the thick bushes. The first time I'd entered the maze I'd gotten lost and it had taken me an hour to find my way back out. I knew I could have just flown out, but I was determined to find my own way. Now, the path was as familiar to me as walking up to my room in the house.

I finally made it to the center of the labyrinth, which was a rectangular clearing about twenty square feet wide. I sat and ran my hand through the cool green grass. A small rabbit hopped out from underneath the nearest shrub and stopped in front of me, twitching his nose and moving his ears to pick up any sounds. Reaching out slowly, I began to stroke the rabbit's ears as I drifted off into my trance.

My thoughts always strayed to the prince and the strange connection I could feel in me. It was like a cord, one which if I focused on hard enough could be followed to him. But that was impossible, or it should have been. I also felt a second connection to someone or something, but I couldn't figure out what it was or what it meant.

If he was my mate, then why had I been alone as a wolf for so long? Why had he not found me until now? If he was really my mate then he should have been able to find me twenty years ago, or more. And why couldn't I remember anything?!

I had no idea how long I'd been a wolf because my mind had deteriorated into simple animal urges and instincts at some point and I would still be there if it hadn't been for Selene finding me and rehabilitating me. I knew that I'd gone through several generations of one wolf pack before leaving them for a new one and going through several additional generations with that pack, but I couldn't count the number of years. I was almost afraid to. I did and didn't want to know how old I was. I looked about twenty, but preternaturals age much slower than humans and in varying scales depending upon the race.

Maybe the prince didn't want me? No, I couldn't believe that. It hurt just thinking that.

I still vividly remembered the goddess, or Sidhe woman as I understood now, who was my earliest memory. I had tried to find her again and the place we had been at, but was unsuccessful.

My irritation was growing and the rabbit's fur twitched beneath my tense hands. My stomach growled and for a fleeting moment I thought about eating the rabbit.

"Chandra?" Theseus called.

"In here," I answered softly as I shooed the rabbit away, closed my eyes and started humming softly to meditate.

I felt his wolf as he sat down in front of me. It was strange to be able to *feel* someone like I did now. Had the interaction with the werewolf prince unlocked some of my powers?

I opened my eyes and asked, "How did you find me?"

He tapped his nose. "Scent trail. Are you feeling well?" he asked softly.

"Headache," I whispered. "I hope Blu returns with news from the Council soon."

"Do you know when your dragon friend will return?"

"No. It depends on how quickly the Council makes a decision."

"Would you like to go for a run?" he asked cheerfully.

I shook my head. "No, I think I'd just like to sit here for a moment." I started humming again and slowly slipped back into my meditative trance.

At least I was in my trance until a cold hand touched my face. "The dark approaches. Fire will consume and restore, happiness and pain must be experienced collectively. Death for three will be the end."

I opened my eyes and looked up at Margenta. Her eyes were opened wide, but only the whites were showing. A prophecy. Margenta was using her power of prophecy on me. "Who are the three?" I asked softly so as not to awaken her from her trance.

"Starlight, twice stars and moons. Those are the three."

"When?"

No response.

"Can the path be altered?"

"Fate can always be changed. Decisions must be made. But

the death is unchangeable. Death requires the lives and Death will not be denied."

"Can another life be traded?"

"Death will not be denied the three. A decision will be made, but not by thee."

Margenta's eyes closed and then she gasped in a huge lungful of breath and dropped to her knees beside me. "What happened?" she asked.

"Prophecy," I whispered.

Her eyes widened and she looked at me in horror. "No, oh no. Chandra I am sorry."

I smiled and patted her hand reassuringly. "Your Sight is a gift and I thank you for using it on me. You should take a lavender bath to calm yourself."

She nodded and walked on wobbly legs out of the rose garden.

"I need to relay this to the ones who sent me," Theseus said.

I nodded and stood, brushing my backside off. "I need to seek Selene's advice as well."

"Are you alright?" he asked, concern evident in his voice and eyes.

I smiled. "Yes, I have heard many doom prophecies since coming here. I expected one day to hear my own."

He didn't seem convinced, but he left. I sagged to the ground and held my head in my hands. Why me? Why now? What the hell did it mean?

"Are you alright, Sister?"

I looked up and took Selene's extended hand. "No."

"Margenta came to me very distressed. Would you care to enlighten me as to what has happened?"

I exhaled and asked, "Could we go to your office first?"

Selene smiled and put her arm around my shoulders. "Certainly. And when we get there, I will brew you some relaxing tea."

"A shot of whiskey might be better."

Selene laughed, and my despair lightened slightly. She could always lift my mood. Of course, since she said I was surrounded by despair and darkness, that wasn't a difficult task. We walked into the main building and to her office in the east wing on the first floor. I sat down and watched Selene boil water and add leaves. She waved her hand and a pen and a piece of paper appeared in front of me. "Write down the prophecy and any answers she gave you to questions you asked."

I did as she asked and then flipped the paper around so that she could read it when she sat down. She set a cup of steaming tea on the desk in front of me and then sat down in her chair. I sipped my tea and looked around the room. The walls were painted black and aside from the desk and three chairs, only a small overhead light adorned the room. It was the perfect room for a witch to perform spells and meditate in privacy.

Selene's cup shattered as it fell to the floor, making me jump up out of my chair.

"Selene?"

She bent down and started picking up the broken pieces. "I'm alright, Chandra. I'm sorry I startled you." Our eyes met and she swallowed nervously. "Her prophecies have never been wrong."

I plopped down in the chair and sighed. "I know." I could smell Selene's fear and it made me worry. I'd never known the witch to be afraid. "Selene, why are you so frightened?" I asked.

"I need to do some research. You should return to your room and rest. I'm sure this has taken a lot out of you." She stood and walked to the door, opening it for me.

I had never been dismissed by Selene like this before. "Very well," I whispered as I walked past her.

I went to my room and sat on my bed. My room was small, just big enough for my dresser and bed, but it had its own bathroom and since only I lived in it, it was fine for me. It was like a little den where I was safe and could curl up in the dark, away from all of the scary things which hunted when the light disappeared.

Divinations were always tricky to decipher because sometimes they meant exactly what they said while other times they were metaphors. Plus, you couldn't figure out what it meant until it was happening and by then it was too late.

I could feel Theseus' approach before he walked in. He stopped in the doorway and looked at me with a carefully neutral expression on his face. "What did Selene say?"

I was still unaffected by his handsome appearance, which was strange. It seemed unnatural for a woman not to be affected by him. I could see that many of the witches were, so why wasn't I?

"Nothing. What did the werewolf prince say?" Just the thought of him sent my heart twisting. How could a man I didn't know affect me like this?

"He said quite a few swear words and then broke a few things. Then his second-in-command took the phone and told me that they would contact us if they deciphered anything." He sat on the bed beside me and wrapped his arms around my shoulders. "Are you alright?"

I scoffed. "I'm great. I'm being lied to by someone I thought was my friend. I discover a man who may or may not be my mate and who may or may not have abandoned me. And now one of my sisters foretells a prophecy that, I think, talks about my death." I flopped backwards onto the bed and growled. "Life is great."

"Let's go outside and play," Theseus suggested.

I shook my head. "No, I think I just want to sleep."

"We could fight if you wanted. I might even let you win once."

I smiled despite my mood and sat up. "You're on."

We walked out of the house with my sisters staring after me with solemn expressions. I gritted my teeth and followed Theseus out to the garden. Theseus stopped and turned to face me, his face serious as he stretched his legs and arms. "Are you ready?"

I smiled and charged forward, trying my hardest to hit him. He dodged left and right, keeping me at bay. I managed to clip his chin and then he was attacking me. I dodged his attacks, but my concentration wavered as I watched him attack. His style was familiar. I had an extreme case of déjà vu as I tried to remember who fought like him. My head throbbed from the effort, making me stumble and drop to my knees. I clutched my head as the pain increased.

Theseus dropped down beside me and rested his hand on my shoulder, trying to comfort me, and as he did so, we heard a noise above.

Blu roared overhead and wind pressed me down to the ground as he landed over me. I heard Theseus growl, but I was in too much pain to tell him to shut up. Blu placed his snout against my head and hummed, vibrating my entire body. After a moment, the pain in my head eased and then disappeared.

Blu growled again at Theseus and then nuzzled me gently. "Are you alright, Hatchling?"

I stood slowly. "Yes." I remained silent until I was sure that I could stand on my own. "Did the Council give you a decision?"

He muttered as his stomach growled. "First, do you have you any meat?"

Two witches who had been watching our garden play brought out a cow and Blu gulped it down. I waited until he was done licking his lips before asking again, "What did the Council decree?"

Blu looked at Theseus who was standing a few yards away. "How long will it take for your leader to make the journey to the Lair?"

Theseus answered quickly, "Two days."

Blu huffed. "Then you best notify him now that he needs to start his journey.

Theseus bowed and hurried into the house. "Blu! What is going on?" I asked in exasperation.

Blu flicked his tongue out in annoyance. "Your agitation is understandable, Hatchling, but you best remember your place when meeting the Council."

I bit my tongue and bowed my head, "I apologize, Draco-Blu. I have been in pain lately."

Blu pressed his nose against my head and exhaled. The sweet smell of his breath surrounded me as he used his magic to quickly view my memories of the time since he left. He snorted and pulled his nose back. "I see. Well, you and I will begin our journey to the Council and assuming all of the conditions are met, they will assist you in regaining your memory."

They'd agreed! I was finally going to find out who I was! "Wait, what conditions?"

Blu shook his head. "They are not conditions for you so you need not worry until we arrive. Pack your things and let us head out."

I wanted to argue, but there are two types of beings you never argue with, vampires and dragons. So, I hurried up to my room and packed what little clothes and things I had. Theseus came into my room and watched me silently. I finished packing and turned to see him looking sad and fearful. "What is it, Theseus?"

He swallowed and smiled. "Just worried that once you regain your prior memories that you won't remember your time with me and we won't be friends."

I wrapped my arms around him and kissed his cheek. "You will always be my friend. You are the only one like me."

Theseus rubbed the back of his neck. "Actually, there are quite a few others like us."

I gaped at him. "What? When were you going to tell me?"

He shrugged. "I was told not to tell you too much. You'll meet the others once your memory is back though."

"How many others?"

Theseus whispered, "Hundreds."

Hundreds of wolf halfbreeds! How come I had never seen them? How come I didn't know they even existed?

"Let's go, hatchling!" Blu called from outside.

I pointed at Theseus. "You and I are going to talk about this later."

He smiled. "Of course."

I headed down the stairs into the main living room and found all of the witches gathered. The children were teary eyed, and the adults seemed more worried than sad. "This isn't goodbye. I'm still a part of this coven and will return. I promise," I said to the gathered women.

The children I'd grown to love took their turns giving me hugs and kissing me goodbye. Each of the witches bade me farewell and wished me luck. Selene stood at the exit and handed me a talisman. "This will hide your scent and Theseus' long enough for you to make it to the Lair. Be strong, Chandra, and return to me whole."

I hugged her and kissed her cheek. "I love you, Selene. Thank you for helping me regain my humanity."

Blu set me on his back and I slipped the talisman on. The designs on my skin faded and my hair turned blonde. She had to have put an extreme amount of power into the talisman for it to change my appearance so drastically. I looked at Theseus who was climbing onto Blu's back behind me and blinked. The markings on his skin were gone as well.

Blu roared farewell to the coven and took us up into the sky. The press of wind on my body felt wonderful. I leaned into it and lifted my arms beside me. I looked back at Theseus to find him sitting with his eyes closed and a smile on his lips as he enjoyed the wind on him as well.

"How long will it take us to get to the Lair?" I asked Blu.

"Two days. I will travel as far as I can the first night. I fear staying on the ground too long with two halfbreeds, even with Selene's talisman on you."

Theseus sighed longingly. "Someday the vampires won't have the power to make us hide in fear."

Blu laughed. "Yes, little halfbreed hatchlings, someday soon you will restore the balance."

We flew in silence until the sun rose and brightened the sky. Blu landed near a river, and we all slurped at the water. My nose twitched as I caught the scent of a deer, but before I could turn to chase after it, Theseus was already bounding into the forest.

I growled, yanked my clothes and talisman off and then charged after him. He stood in wolf form over a large buck, his muzzle stained red from taking it down.

I changed forms and walked forward, growling softly. *Step aside.*

Theseus dropped his head and backed away slowly. *Of course. I simply wanted to take it down for you.*

I turned so that I could watch Theseus then tore into the deer and ate until I was full. Once my stomach was full and my anger sated, I walked a few feet away and lay down to lick my muzzle and paws clean. Something seemed familiar about this situation, but during the years I'd spent as a wolf I'd gone on many hunts with the small wolf packs, so I pushed the thought away and changed forms. "I'm going to the river to bathe."

I jogged back towards Blu and then past him to the river. I shivered at the cold water and Blu plugged one nostril, snorting a jet of fire into the river around me, warming it instantly. I sighed happily and then started tossing him the fish which he'd killed in the process. I washed my body and then caught a few more fish for Blu before walking to the shore. I closed my eyes and called to the flame of power which resided deep within me. The flame brightened and then purple fire covered my body. I held the flame around me long enough to dry my body and then dressed and put the talisman back on.

"Your control over your fire has improved," Blu said as he used one of his large talons to pick at bones in his teeth.

I finger-combed my hair and smiled. "I had been working

on it daily. The last thing I need is to offend the Council by accidentally shooting a flame at them."

Blu laughed. "Yes, that would be considered a grave insult."

I smiled. "Fira didn't like it much when I shot his nose with my fire yesterday."

Blu laughed, shaking the ground and me. "It was a good tactic, but it's never pleasant to have foreign fire on you."

"Have you learned to use your fire to deflect another's?" asked Theseus as he walked to the river and cleaned the blood from his body.

I watched him as he cleaned and grew angry at my incapacity to be interested in him. "Yes, I have. Have you?"

Theseus stood up and red flames surrounded him in a mini tornado. "As you can see."

I envisioned fire covering my hands and purple flames covered them instantly. I formed two giant streams of fire from my hands to his body and watched as the blue and purple flames swirled together and then my purple disappeared from his body. Theseus inhaled as he prepared to attack me back, but Blu snorted two twin jets of blue flames between us. "That is enough, hatchlings. We must rest."

"I was just playing," I grumbled.

Blu sighed at me and lay down. I climbed between his leg and body, underneath his wing and curled up into a ball. Theseus cleared his throat, and I smiled at him. "Come on. Blu won't mind if you lie with me here. He's large enough."

Theseus smiled and climbed beside me, curling around me.

"Good night, hatchlings. May your dreams be pleasant," Blu whispered as we drifted off to sleep against him.

The rain poured like a giant waterfall down my face as I scanned the forest. I wiped at the rain, but nothing helped. I put my hands over my eyes and screamed in frustration. I tensed as a wolf howled nearby, answering my scream. I walked backwards into the cave, pressing my back against the wall. My heart hammered against my chest, threatening to break through. I wiped the water from my eyes and stared at the black opening of the cave. Lightning flashed, allowing me to see outside, and my entire body stilled. A large black wolf stood in the doorway sniffing the ground. The wolf turned its head towards me and sniffed three times quickly. I tried to slow my breathing, but the adrenaline was pumping too quickly to allow it. The wolf walked into the cave and whimpered. I shook my head and closed my eyes. The sound of bones snapping and popping echoed in the cave. I hugged myself tighter, fear consuming my rational thought. A familiar male voice whispered, "It's alright. I won't hurt you. I'm your mate."

I woke up gasping for air, and my head throbbed in pain. Theseus whined beside me, and I realized he was now in wolf form.

"Are you alright, Hatchling?" Blu asked. "I feel that you are in pain."

I groaned. "My head...hurts."

Blu placed his nose against my head and exhaled. In a matter of seconds, the pain was gone, and I relaxed against Blu and Theseus.

"Thank you," I said as I fell back asleep.

Morning came faster than I wanted. I felt drained, emotionally and physically. The pain in my head was still present as was the pain in my entire body due to the connection with the werewolf prince. I felt it stronger than ever and knew I needed to see him soon, or I felt as though I would break.

Blu and Theseus ate quickly and after I forced down a few bites of food, we set off into the air again. Blu sang softly in the language of the dragons as we flew and after a few minutes I started to fall asleep again. Theseus wrapped his arms around me to keep me from falling off and I let Blu's magical song put me to sleep, healing the parts of me that it could.

I WOKE when Blu started rumbling beneath me. I recognized his angry growl and was instantly alert. Theseus stood on the ground beside Blu in wolf form, his fur puffed out as he snarled at something in the distance. I started to climb off of Blu's back, but he snapped, "Stay there."

I frowned. "What is it?"

"I landed to get water for you both and a group of strange vampires surrounded us," Blu said.

"Why don't we just fly away then?" I asked softly.

"Because we have archers with us," said a melodious voice which sounded vaguely familiar. A man with white skin and golden designs stepped out from the tree line. I didn't need to be near him to recognize that he was Sidhe.

"What do you want?" I asked. "And why are you working with vampires?"

The man smiled and there was something nagging at the back of my mind about him. He looked familiar somehow. "I was sent to intercept you."

Theseus changed forms and let his wings out. "You will not take her, traitor."

Blu roared and shifted his back foot. The signal. Blu had taught me this signal the first day we met. I screamed in rage and used all of the power I could without draining myself to send a ring of sunshine outwards away from my body.

Vampires screamed and disintegrated in fifty puffs of ash. The Sidhe roared and jumped up to come at me, but Blu and Theseus shot him with their fire, forcing him to protect himself and drop to the ground.

Theseus jumped onto Blu's back as Blu continued to spray the man with fire and then we took off into the air and zoomed away. I looked back, but the man did not follow us, though we all knew this wasn't the last that we'd seen of him.

"How did they know where we were? How could they have known we would be heading this way?" I asked with a frown.

Theseus sighed. "That would probably be my fault."

Blu's head whipped around, murderous intent in his eyes. "You have two seconds to explain before I chomp off your head."

Theseus looked at me with pleading eyes. "I made a call to the werewolf prince, but spoke quickly before asking if he was alone. He has an ally who is a vampire, but sometimes his ally has minions around him who are not loyal. I should have asked first if it was safe to speak, but we were in a rush and…I am sorry."

Blu spoke rapidly in the language of the dragons, which meant he was saying harsh things he didn't want me to hear.

"You should be more careful next time," I said softly, "Apparently, I'm wanted by the vampires."

Finally, we reached the end of the landmass and flew out over the water. The ocean spread out before us in a seemingly endless expanse. The winds blew the scent of salt up to us, making my nose tingle and me sneeze. The sea was powerful and silent. It was eerie and yet reassuring. The only difference from the preternatural takeover and from when the humans ruled, is that now the ocean was *much* cleaner.

We flew in silence for the next two hours, passing over the sea and mountains until we finally came to the Lair. The mountain before us was the largest in the world, its peak over twenty-nine thousand feet high. It was also hollow. The dragons used their magic to hollow out the mountain yet maintain its stability.

The entrance was over fifteen thousand feet from the base and only accessible by air. It was also always covered in snow which made it a massive sight of splendor. Blu told me that there used to be other mountains around it, but the dragons thought they made a route for unwanted visitors so the dragons destroyed all of the mountains within a one-hundred-mile radius, leaving the behemoth dragon's nest by itself.

Blu approached the mountain slowly, making a wide arc so the guards had time to come to him and check him out.

Two dragons roared and then swooped down from above where they'd been making lazy patrolling circles. The first dragon was green and large, but still smaller than Blu.

"Welcome Draco-Blu. We are honored to escort you in," said the green dragon.

The second dragon, a gold colored dragon, glided besides Blu's left side. "Hail, leader. I am honored to be in your presence yet again." He was closer to Blu's size and as I recalled, one of Blu's friends.

Blu hummed respectfully, confirming my belief. "I am happy to see you again my friend."

The golden dragon tilted his head and flicked his tongue out, trying to catch my scent. "You must be the girl Draco-Blu is so fond of."

I bowed my head out of respect and then smiled at him. "I am Chandra, friend of the dragons."

The green dragon asked, "How are you faring at the moment?"

I bowed to the other dragon and said, "I am doing alright. My pulse is faster than normal and there is a pain in my head and heart, but nothing too serious."

The dragons glided as they approached the entrance and then formed a single file line with the golden dragon first, then Blu and then the green dragon. They landed inside the opening, which was only wide enough for one dragon with his wings fully extended to land at a time. Blu followed his friend through a pitch-black tunnel which made Theseus and me growl nervously. I hated confined spaces, especially ones under the ground. My head throbbed as I recalled walking down a narrow staircase underground with a man in a situation very similar to this.

I screamed in pain as I tried to recall his name or what he looked like.

Blu stepped out of the darkness and into the open mountain where the dragons lived. We stood on a ledge which dropped off to the bottom of the mountain. Rock outcroppings jutted out every twenty feet or so which served as nests for the dragons along the walls of the mountain. The nests were scattered along the full height and circumference of the mountain's walls.

Theseus grabbed me and jumped off of Blu's back, being careful to keep me from the edge and set me down in front of Blu. Blu and the golden dragon pressed their noses to my head and started humming.

The man in the staircase was connected to me. I recalled being able to speak telepathically with him, which was abnormal. I had been afraid, and he started glowing. He glowed because he was a Sidhe! He was tall and he had markings on his upper body...

"Hatchling!" Blu yelled. "Release the memory! Release it before it tears you apart!"

Release it? Why would I release it when I was so close? I could almost see his face. I could… Pain ripped through my body and stole the breath from my lungs, not even allowing me to scream.

Theseus bit my arm, and my eyes flew open, releasing the memory from my grasp. Blu and his friend hummed loudly, their magic wrapping around me in a soft whirlwind. The pain eased and then disappeared, allowing me to breathe.

"Speak to me, Chandra," Theseus whispered, "Please, say something."

I lay in stunned silence a moment and then whispered, "Ow."

The three dragons and Theseus exhaled in relief simultaneously, ruffling my hair with their combined releases of air. Blu rested his muzzle on my chest and whispered, "You need to be careful, Hatchling. That was too close."

I patted his muzzle reassuringly and then stood up slowly. "I'm sorry."

Theseus cleared his throat and the dragons turned to look at him. "Would it be alright if I flew down with you instead of riding?"

My eyes widened, and I looked at Blu hopefully. "Please, Draco-Blu. It has been so long since I've soared," I pleaded.

Blu locked eyes with his friend a moment as they communicated telepathically and then nodded. "You may follow us down to the floor level." Blu looked at me with concern and asked, "Are you sure you're alright to fly?"

I smiled and nodded vigorously. "Yes!"

Blu and the other two dragons sprang up and away from the ledge, extended their wings and soared over the giant expanse of the open mountain. Theseus pulled his shirt off over his head and then walked behind me, tearing open slits in my shirt so I could let my wings out while still keeping my shirt intact and covering my upper body.

I walked a few steps away from him and closed my eyes, calming my mind and body. Power flowed within the mountain and it generously lent me energy. I pictured my back and imagined my wings sliding from the two slits and expanding outwards. My back pulsed and then my wings were free. I opened my eyes and marveled at the colors of my body.

Theseus grunted and I watched as his body glowed and then his wings released. He smiled at me and then launched himself from the ledge.

I squatted down and then jumped up as high as I could, letting out a victorious cry of glee as I soared. I zipped past the others and made a circle around the entire mountain. If my calculation was correct, the area of the base of the mountain was at least twenty-five hundred square feet. Theseus flew after me and then folded his wings in and plummeted down towards the bottom. I followed close behind him but pulled up early to circle one more time before landing on my feet on the stone floor.

Blu landed beside me and roared happily. If I smiled any wider, my face would surely split. Mid-smile, I glanced at the floor of the mountain more carefully. Blu had described the mountain for me before, but it was incredible to witness first-hand. The ground was solid marble and several large tents were set up along the outer edge of the floor level.

"Who lives in the tents?" I asked curiously.

"Friends of the dragons when they visit," the golden dragon answered.

I turned to face him and said, "I must apologize for my

rudeness. I have forgotten to ask what I may call you."

The golden dragon's lips pulled back slightly as he gave me a dragon smile. "Friends call me Fafnir."

I frowned as I recalled the name from a story I'd heard. "Doesn't that mean greed?"

Fafnir and Blu laughed loudly. Fafnir nodded. "Gold is not only my coloring, but my favorite treasure."

I smiled. "Aw, so your treasure holds more than just jewels and virgins waiting to be devoured?"

Blu snorted. "He wishes he had virgins again."

Fafnir sighed. "I do miss those days. Humans were so much tastier before they developed so many chemicals."

I turned to the green dragon and bowed. "I have not forgotten you. What may I call you?"

"I am Ryuu."

I smiled. "It is a pleasure to meet you Ryuu and Fafnir. I am honored."

Ryuu and Fafnir dipped their heads. "We are honored to meet you as well, Hatchling," they said in unison.

I'd heard Blu and Fira speak in unison before, but it was strange to hear other dragons do it as well. Blu said it was because of their telepathy. Sometimes they finished sentences for each other as well.

"Chandra," said five voices at once.

I turned and watched as the five oldest dragons, so worn with age that they rarely flew and if they did fly, only made it as far as the first nests two hundred feet overhead, walked towards me. They were all bi-colored, the only multicolored dragons I'd ever seen before. Were they more powerful because they were bi-colored or had they become bi-colored after becoming the Council? I wasn't sure since Blu never talked about it.

The dragons stopped a hundred feet away and held my gaze. I walked away from Blu and Theseus and dropped to the ground on my knees and bowed until my forehead touched the marble. I trembled inside, but I held my body tight as I bowed. I would not show fear to the Council. "It is an honor to have an audience with you, Council of Dragons."

"We are pleased to finally meet the hatchling of Draco-Blu," they answered in unison again. "Please stand, friend of the dragons, and be easy in our presence. You have nothing to fear from us."

I stood up and bowed my head politely. "Thank you."

"Please let us look upon your face."

I took off the talisman to reveal my true face. The dragons stared at me and hummed in harmony as they each used their magic in sync to examine me.

I felt like a tuning fork that had been flicked. Their powers vibrated against me, infiltrating my mind and body. I tried to relax despite my fear so as not to disrupt their spell.

Images of events I did not remember started to play across my closed eyelids and made me cry out in pain. I fell to the ground on my side as the pain blacked out my vision. The images stopped and the dragons' magic dissipated.

"You are not ready to face this on your own. We must wait for him to come," the Council said.

Theseus picked me up from the ground where I was laying and carried me as he followed Blu towards one of the tents.

"Draco-Blu, I…" I began.

"Quiet. You must sleep and wait, Hatchling," Blu said with concern and worry evident in his voice.

I closed my eyes and a smile spread across my face as I whispered, "I can feel him coming."

Blu snorted in my face and the world went dark.

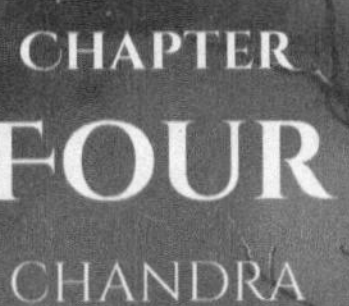

CHAPTER

FOUR

CHANDRA

"I want to see her!" yelled a familiar deep, commanding male voice.

"She is resting," said Blu, growling.

"I'm awake," I whispered because I knew both would hear me.

Blu stuck his head into the opening of the small tent Where I lay. "How do you feel?" he asked.

"Like I got stepped on by a dragon."

Blu laughed. "You would not be alive if that were true, Hatchling."

"Please, I would just like to see her," said the werewolf prince.

Blu sighed. "Are you well enough to have visitors?"

I smiled at Blu and stood up slowly. "I am. Thank you for your concern."

Blu rumbled affectionately at me, much like a feline would purr.

I changed quickly and then took a deep breath for courage

55

just as he stepped into the tent. He was even more handsome than I remembered.

He had started to move towards me but stopped and clenched his hands into fists. "How are you feeling?"

"I've been better," I admitted.

"Did they hurt you?" he asked through gritted teeth.

I frowned at him. "Did who hurt me?"

His eyes flicked to the side. "The Dragon Council."

I frowned at him. "They were trying to help me. I am sure they did not mean to harm me."

Theseus walked into the tent with a tray of food but stopped when he saw the prince. "I...I'm sorry. I didn't know you were here." Theseus dropped his head in submission and started to leave.

"Wait," I said. "Is that food for me?"

Theseus looked at the tray and then smiled nervously. "Yes, sorry. I'll just leave it."

I felt the prince watching us as I walked to Theseus and took the tray from his hands. I kissed Theseus' cheek and smiled at him. "Thank you."

The prince growled softly behind me, but made no movement besides that.

I ignored him and walked outside to eat beside Blu who still stood guard outside of my tent. Blu moved his tail so I could sit on it while leaning against him to eat as I'd done many times before. I sat down and patted his side before eating the meats and fruits on the tray.

"When will I speak to the Council?" the prince asked. His shoulders were tense, and his eyes glowed with magic.

Why was he so angry? Even if he was my mate, I hadn't done anything that was considered inappropriate.

"As soon as she is ready," Blu answered.

The prince started to move towards me, but Blu growled and wrapped his tail protectively around me, lifting me up to my feet.

The prince squatted down in an attack stance and changed his hands to paws.

I smacked Blu's tail. "You're being rude and possessive, both of you, and I don't like it."

Blu exhaled smoke. "I apologize. I did not mean to offend you."

The prince changed his hands back and his eyes returned to normal. "I'm sorry. I am not usually like this."

"The Council will see you both now," said the combined voices of the Council who were walking towards the center of the mountain.

I walked next to Blu, but felt the prince behind me like a weight on my back. We stopped in front of the Council and I dropped to the ground in a bow. "Thank you for seeing us, Council," I said as humbly as I could. I stood back up and rested a hand on Blu's shoulder for support.

"We have spoken to the Prince of Werewolves and know he has spoken the truth."

Then he was my mate! How? Why were we separated?

The Council continued, "But we cannot perform the recognition spell until the other man you are tied to has arrived."

"He should be here any minute," said the Prince.

I looked at the Council. "Wait. What do you mean the other man I am tied to? I thought you said that the Prince was telling the truth about me being his mate!"

"You are my mate, but you are also bound to another. It was an emergency action done to save your life," answered the Prince.

"But I do not regret it," said a voice like wind chimes.

I knew that voice, and I definitely knew the language with which that voice would normally speak. Sidhe. The man behind me was a Sidhe and judging by the presence I felt, a very powerful one.

What had I done in my life to warrant the attention of the Prince of Werewolves and the… I turned around and one look at his face released a torrent of memories. I screamed in pain as I saw the Sidhe holding me while I was in pain, saw him walk with me down a dark staircase and reassuring me with his presence. Heard his voice in my head whispering that he loved me…

I screamed again and my eyes flew open. Blu was lying across me, humming and singing in the magic of dragons. The pain in my head was subsiding, but my heart felt like it was going to explode. I turned my head and found the Sidhe and werewolf princes being held back by dragons. Yes, that was who he was, a prince. Wow. Two princes?!

The princes looked at me with fear and anger. Were they mad at me or with the dragons holding them back?

"Blu, I think you can let me up now," I whispered. The Dragon Council growled and I realized that I'd slipped and addressed him informally. "I'm sorry, I meant to say Draco-Blu. Please forgive my offense."

Blu let me up, but pressed his nose to my head. "I accept your apology. You're in much pain still though. Perhaps you should lie still while I heal you?"

"You cannot heal this pain, Draco-Blu." I looked at the princes. "They are the cause of the pain and I believe only they know how I can fix it."

Blu lunged across the opening and pinned each of the

princes to the ground under his talons. "What have you done to her?"

I rushed to him and put my face in front of his. "No! You misunderstand! Don't harm them!"

"Let them up, Draco-Blu," said the Council.

Blu hissed at the princes and let them up, but not before pulling me back against his chest with his head away from the princes.

The princes both began to glow incandescently. "Step away from her," they said eerily in unison.

"We will begin our discussion now," said the Council distracting everyone.

I stepped away from Blu and walked to stand in the center of the circle of dragons. "I am ready and will humbly accept whatever decision you give."

"You are a valued friend of the dragons and we treasure your acceptance of us," they said to me.

The two princes came to stand on either side of me and I had to fight the urge to reach out and touch them. The Council looked at the Sidhe prince. "You are unknown to us, which is neither good nor bad as we are neither good nor bad, thus we are willing to assist you if you meet our small request."

"Anything for her," he said without hesitation.

The Council then turned to the werewolf prince and their mood darkened. "You are very well known by us. You almost destroyed the race of dragons, you and the vampire prince. You are no friend of ours."

"I will do anything you ask to make amends for the devastation I caused and for my ignorant and childish actions," he said quietly.

"You are no friend of ours and there is nothing you can do

to make amends for what you have done, but we love the hatchling you are mated to and thus we will agree to ease the suffering in her if you agree to a test to prove your loyalty."

"Anything," he answered without pause.

The Council was silent a moment and then they said, "In addition to one task we will divulge later, you must retrieve the lost dragon egg."

I gasped and Blu snorted in surprise.

The werewolf prince asked, "Would this be the green egg which the vampires found eighty years ago?"

The Council looked at him suspiciously. "Yes, that is the egg we speak of. We have heard rumor that the King of Vampires has it in his possession and plans to hatch it and control the dragon within. We must not let this happen."

"So, if I get the egg and hand it to you, you will help Ar… Chandra regain her memories?" he asked.

The Council shook with anger. Why was he asking them to repeat themselves?

"Yes, if you hand the egg to us, intact and safe, and pass one more test, we will assist the hatchling in regaining her memories and thus returning her to you as she was before she was stolen from you."

The werewolf prince nodded. "Alright, deal. I will need Ach…the Sidhe prince to fly down to the bottom of the mountain to assist me, is this alright?" The Council nodded and the werewolf prince smiled. "Great. We will be back as soon as we can with your egg."

The Council was eerily silent as they talked amongst themselves, probably pondering what he had up his sleeve.

I turned to the princes. "You do realize that the King of the Vampires could capture you and kill you, right?"

The princes both smiled at me, their smiles bizarrely similar. If I didn't know better, I'd say that they were brothers. I wanted to get closer to the werewolf prince to smell him, but decided better of it and planted my feet on the ground.

The werewolf prince asked, "Are you worried about my safety?"

I stepped back and then glared at him. "I was just saying that it seems like a lot of trouble to go to for a girl who doesn't remember you." Both princes winced as though I'd struck them. I hadn't meant to be so harsh, but he was rude and I didn't like it.

The werewolf prince came to stand a few inches from me and whispered, "I would face the entire Flight of Dragons to have you back in my arms and have you remember the times we've spent together. I would cut off my arm and give it to the dragons as payment if they would accept it. You are the only important thing in my life and I will face a hundred Vampire Kings before I let something as simple as death make me hesitate in getting you back."

The conviction and feeling in his voice were overpowering and I would have fallen if not for Blu's tail catching me. "She needs to rest."

The werewolf prince smiled at me and said, "I'll be back. You don't need to worry about me."

I groaned as a memory of a weaker, non-magical me stood on the porch of someone's house watching the werewolf prince leave somewhere and say those exact words to me. Blu whisked me away from the princes and into my tent before I could say anything else. He laid his head on me and sang until I fell asleep.

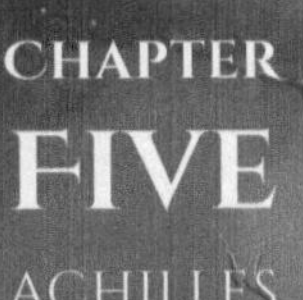

CHAPTER

FIVE

ACHILLES

I couldn't believe that we had finally found her. She looked even more beautiful than I remembered and yet I could see that she was not herself. The need to touch her was incredible, but I resisted so as not to cause her pain. She was so strong and yet so fragile since she had not found herself yet. I gripped Ares under the arms and jumped out of the Lair, letting the wind catch us.

"Could you please *not* jump." Ares hissed as his heartbeat quickened.

"I had forgotten that you are afraid of heights," I said.

He growled. "I'm not afraid of heights, I'm afraid of you dropping me."

We landed on the ground and I patted his shoulder. "I wouldn't drop you, Brother."

Ares grunted, cleared his throat and then howled as loudly as he could. I wished I could see the process of his vocal chords and throat changing shape when he went from a human's throat to a wolf's throat. Although I doubted slicing a man's throat in half to watch would then allow the process to complete.

A bat screeched nearby and I smiled. Victor loved being a bat when he could. I think he just liked being smaller and able to fly.

A small black bat came to hover in front of us and then changed into a six-foot-tall, black eyed man. If you were human you might think he was simply imposing, but it was just his raw, incredible power. Victor was one of the few vampires I genuinely trusted and did not fear. He shook out his body and then looked at me with a smile, showing just the tips of his fangs. "I do enjoy being smaller and being able to fly."

I pointed at him. "Stay out of my head."

Ares sighed. "If only that were possible."

We'd known each other so long that most times we knew what the other was thinking without the use of telepathic abilities, so Victor's abilities were not as intrusive as they once were.

Being one thousand years old made years seem like a human's minutes, but the last one hundred years had felt like a lifetime. I had finally revealed myself to Artemis in Lyngvi, trying to claim her, only to come up against Ares and the bond they had already developed. Then, after many fights and binding her to save her from Hera, I had told her that I loved her and showed her my memories only to have her taken from me by my mother. I understand why Hera had done it, but it didn't make the pain at being separated from Artemis any easier. Especially when we hadn't been able to find her where Hera claimed to have left her.

And now Ares had been the first to find her, the first to make contact with her. I hated that he had been able to find her first, but I could not direct that hate at him. I'd watched him suffer each night with only Koda there to console him as he lost the ability to hold shape and turned into a wolf. Not being able to maintain shape was something very uncommon for the Prince of the Werewolves. Every night he dreamed of her being taken and then turned into a wolf, howling his grief until he passed out from weariness.

A wolf's grieving howl was the most eerie and heart wrenching sound I'd ever heard. It made it that much worse to feel the same pain and sorrow echoed in my own heart. My soul howled right along with his as we ached to see and touch her.

The day Ares had come back from the town to confirm it was her, he had seemed defeated instead of happy. Now, seeing her and knowing she did not recognize us and did not feel for us as she had when we'd last seen her, hurt incredibly. She had been the love of my life since I had first seen her, and she had no clue who I was.

What had she been doing since we last saw her? Had she found a mate? Had she slept with someone else? What if she had a family? Could we really give her back her memories if she was already happy?

Theseus had said she was living in a witch's coven and that she didn't smell of a man, but it had been a hundred years; she could have mated with a human and had a family between now and then.

The thought of another man touching her made my fists clench and my skin start to glow.

"Achilles," Ares said softly, "It'll be alright."

I turned away from the concern on his face and ground my teeth together. "You have already established a bond with her. Of course, you think it'll be alright. I am, yet again, left to wait."

"Would you like me to answer the questions you were asking yourself a moment ago?" Victor asked me quietly. "I have seen some of her memories and know some of the answers."

It was tempting, extremely tempting, but I shook my head. "No, thank you. I shall wait to hear them from her lips."

Even if I hadn't been bound to her and she hadn't been my match, I wouldn't have been able to leave her or forget her. She was perfect. She was the only woman I wanted. The only one I thought about. She was everything to me.

Ares rested his hand on my shoulder and then turned to Victor. "We need the dragon egg your father has."

"That is the price the Council asked of you?" Victor gaped at us.

Ares smiled. "Yes, well I don't think they knew that you could just pop in and get it and come back."

Victor smiled. "Yes, translocation is a handy ability."

It would have been a much handier ability if he had had it when we were captured one hundred years ago. Of course, we had all learned some new ability which would help us should we be captured again. None of us enjoyed being imprisoned.

Victor closed his eyes, chanted a few words and then disappeared. Ares turned and met my eyes. "She'll remember you too, Achilles. She won't get only the memories of me back."

I sat down on the snow-covered ground and exhaled. "I know, Ares. It's just…"

"Painful," Ares offered.

I laughed bitterly. "Yes, painful. I see the way she looks at you now, even without memories, and it's like being back in Lyngvi again."

Ares sat down beside me and sighed. "I hadn't intentionally set out to find her first, to keep you second. I was just overcome with emotions when seeing her and her not knowing me. She looked so different, but then she yelled at me and I knew that she was still in there. I had to try."

Victor appeared in front of us holding a large green egg. "Got it."

I pointed at the small man latched onto his arm. "Someone grabbed on for the ride."

Victor hissed and handed Ares the egg. "I hate stalkers." He pried the other vampire's teeth from his arm and then snapped his neck.

Ares cradled the egg like a baby. "Let's go, Victor you come with us."

Victor sighed. "I knew you'd get me in trouble at some point. You better hope they don't try to kill me."

Ares smiled. "That would be a shame."

Victor smiled wide enough to flash all of his fangs and then changed into his bat form, squealing as he flew up towards the Lair's entrance.

I extended my wings and smiled. "Life has been entertaining with you two around the last hundred years. Losing Victor's comedic relief might dampen the mood."

Ares laughed. "Let's hope the dragons don't eat the winged rat before we get there."

I jumped up into the sky, flapping my wings to propel me higher. "We'd better hurry then."

SIX

CHANDRA

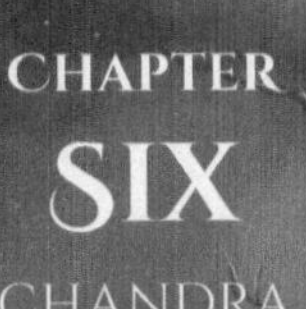

I was really tired of sleeping so much. I woke up with Blu's heavy head still on my chest. "Blu, I need to use the restroom," I said as I pushed at his head.

Blu rumbled something incoherent and pulled his head out of my tent.

After freshening up, I walked outside to find the Council gathered around my two princes. I ran toward them and widened my eyes at the vampire standing in between them. He was tall with black hair and solid black eyes. I'd heard about him before, the vampire prince.

"Please accept my humblest apologies. I was a much more immature man then and very impulsive. I return what is rightfully yours in accordance with the agreement between you and the princes here. I hope you can heal her quickly for all of our sakes."

"I know you, too? What kind of woman was I? Do I even want to know about my former life?" I blinked and shook my head.

The vampire prince turned towards me and I saw several

emotions flit across his face before happiness settled in. "You are even more beautiful than I recall," he whispered as he walked towards me, "and definitely more powerful."

I stepped back from him and then ground my teeth together. "I don't know why you are trying to frighten me, but if those two men are really tied to me in one way or another, then they will not allow you to harm me. Plus, I may seem fragile and *damaged*, but I still possess many powers."

The vampire laughed and the tension eased. "Even without her memories she is still just as assertive and wonderful."

"We are pleased with the return of our egg. We will now give you, Prince of the Werewolves, your final task," said the Council.

"I am ready," said the werewolf prince.

The Council stood in silence a moment and then said, "You must obtain approval from Rhea to continue being mated to this woman."

I gasped in horror.

"Very well. I accept the task," said the werewolf prince without hesitation.

"No!" I yelled. The Council looked at me in shock. I ran to the prince and looked into his eyes. "You can't do this. It's suicide! Please, please don't do this."

"Seeing your worry for me and feeling it from you is greater than anything I've felt in the past hundred years," he said quietly. He picked up a strand of my hair and inhaled deeply. "I will return to you. Nothing will keep me away from you now that I have finally found you."

"Don't go. We can start a life together now. I don't need my memories," I pleaded with him. "I'm not worth anyone's life."

He hugged me against his chest and kissed me fiercely on

the lips. My head throbbed, but I ignored it as I enjoyed the easing of the pain in my heart and felt his love. He pulled back from me and I swore his eyes were misty with tears. "I will come back to you as soon as I can. I'm very powerful so you needn't worry."

I sniffed and wiped at the tears falling down my face. "Your power means nothing against the Mother. I should go. I should be the one who has to risk my life. I should…"

He kissed me again and then rubbed his face against mine, marking me with his delicious scent. "You should stay here and rest. The Sidhe prince will remain so you will not be apart from both of us." He turned to the Council. "May I ask two things?" The Council noddeds. "May I take a helper with me?"

"You may."

He nodded and I caught the vampire prince walking towards us. "My second request is to leave my younger brother here. I do not think it would be good for Ar… Chandra to see him, but I don't want to take him with me."

The Council said, "He may stay while you are on your journey and we will keep him separate from the hatchling." They turned to the Sidhe prince. "In fact, you will all be kept away from her so that she doesn't have any unfortunate episodes while the werewolf prince is away."

The Sidhe prince bowed, but his jaw bulged as he ground his teeth together. "Of course."

The vampire prince sighed. "We'd better not die. I want to live to two thousand years. If I stay your friend I may not live that long though."

The werewolf prince smiled. "Oh come on. You know you're excited to finally get a chance to meet Rhea. Besides, we haven't had a good challenge in a while."

"You're lucky I'm so fond of the two of you," the vampire prince said as he started walking away.

"Don't let him fool you. He's been worried about you as well. He was in an uncontrollable rage when we couldn't find you," the Sidhe prince said with a fond smile on his face.

"How long was I missing?" I asked curiously.

"One hundred and five years," he said without hesitation.

I hadn't known my eyes could open so wide or my mouth. "One hundred years!"

The werewolf prince nodded.

"No wonder it was so hard to control my wolf when Selene found me. I was in wolf form for…" I tried to calculate how long I'd been a wolf, but it was all a blur now. "If what you say is true, that means I was a wolf for around forty-five years!"

The werewolf prince stepped in front of me. "I'm leaving now. I expect you to stay out of trouble." He laughed and shook his head. "Saying that to you is like telling a vampire to stay away from the darkness." He sighed and pressed his forehead against mine. "Stay safe until I return. Please. I could not bear to lose you again."

I inhaled his scent and my hands found their way to his hard, broad chest. "I will be anxiously awaiting your return." I leaned into him and inhaled his scent again, trying to hold it in as long as I could. I wanted some way to keep his scent with me, but before I could ask, he was taking his shirt off and handing it to me. I held it away from my body and smiled at him. "Thank you."

He kissed me quickly on the lips then ran after the vampire prince. "If I don't leave now, I fear I never will."

The vampire prince put his arm around the shorter man's shoulders. "Don't worry, she'll look exactly the same when you get back. That's one of the many perks of mating with preternatural women."

The werewolf prince laughed and shook his head. "Always looking on the bright side, aren't you?"

The vampire laughed and looked up at the dragons in their nests around the Lair. "When you're a child of the darkness, that's the only place you can look."

I took a sniff from the shirt and exhaled softly. "Come back soon."

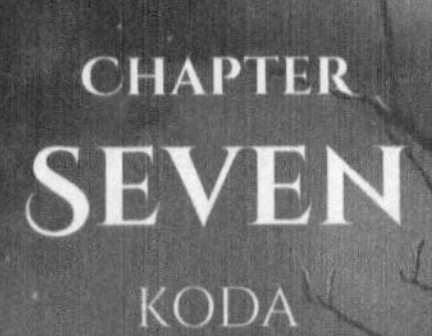

Not only had I been forced to hide in this tent while Ares met with the Council and Artemis, but now I was being forced to wait while he went on a treacherous journey. I had been beside my brother since I was weaned and I did not like being away from him now. I trusted Victor to guard Ares, but was only seventy percent sure that he would give his life for Ares'. I would never even hesitate. Ares was my alpha, my brother, and my only true pack mate since Matt's death.

I had felt sorrow at Matt's betrayal and death, but nothing compared to the pain at Artemis' kidnapping. She was so pure and so sweet, the most perfect female in any race for a million years.

And yet she was not mine to have, except as a pack member. The one kiss we had shared resonated in my skull and burned my heart with longing. I knew she was Ares' and even Achilles' before she would ever be mine, but it didn't stop me from wanting and wishing.

Once she had fully accepted Ares as her *passt genau* I had given up on thoughts of courting her and simply enjoyed her company as part of the pack. Then when she had accepted the challenge from Natasha, there had been a glimmer of hope for me. If she had lost and asked for mercy, I would have left Ares' side to be with her, but her love for Ares was too strong. She had basically died to protect her claim to him.

I wanted to touch her, inhale her scent, bury my nose in her hair and listen to her heart beat. I wanted much and was allowed nothing. It took all of my control not to leave the tent and walk the one hundred yards to hers. She was so close and still so far away.

I'd tried being with other women, even fathering a few children, but it didn't diminish my feelings for Artemis.

I'd just received information from a credible source about the true reason of Matt's treason, but had not been able to discuss it with Ares yet. I stared at the letter in my hands and wished Matt had thought higher of us and had confided his problem in us. Ares and I could have helped him easily and he never would have needed to betray us. Clearly, he did not think much of our skills, which is why he had given in and played the rat.

"What is that?" Achilles asked softly from the stool he was sitting on across the tent from me.

I tossed the note to him and whispered, "Information in regards to Matt's treachery."

Achilles read the note and then looked at me with his neutral face. "Did you tell Ares?"

I shook my head. "There was not an appropriate time to discuss it."

"I am sorry that you have not been allowed to see her," he said quietly as he watched me. "It was not Ares' or my decision, but the Dragon Council's."

It bothered me that he could read me so well, but then

again, he *had* been the first to notice that I was in love with Artemis.

"I know that," I said as I exhaled and ran a hand through my hair. "I just wish the Council wasn't making him go through all this bullshit."

"And that you could have gone with him instead of being left behind," finished Achilles.

I laughed bitterly. "You know me well."

Achilles dipped his head slightly in acknowledgment. "Yes, but I also know that I feel the same way."

This was why I liked Achilles so much. He was the heir to the Sidhe throne and yet he did not hold himself above anyone. Since I could remember, he had been kind to me and had treated me with respect even despite Ares' prior hatred of him. It made matters much easier on me now that Ares had forgiven Achilles and they had dissolved their issues. Although I do not think that would have happened if it had not been for Artemis' kidnapping and our imprisonment together.

We'd had many prison brawls, together and against other prisoners, which had brought us closer. Human women could not understand how fighting brought men together, but after a fight, whether it be against each other or against a common foe, our friendship developed and strengthened.

Victor and Ares' relationship had strengthened, while Achilles and Ares' had developed anew.

"I do not doubt Ares' abilities, but I do not like not being there to protect his back," I admitted.

"Do you doubt Victor?" Achilles asked.

I smiled. "You know as well as I do that Victor will protect Ares as best as he can, but he looks out for himself first, something which I do not."

Achilles' lips drew thin. "I agree."

I looked towards the east, where I could sense Artemis. "It's so frustrating to know she is so near and yet still out of reach."

Achilles sighed loudly. "You're preaching to the choir, brother."

Only he would obtain more kisses from her and, given long enough, possibly even be allowed to mate with her. I would never. I would only be allowed the bond of pack mates and the bond of friendship. Something which I was grateful for, but I craved so much more.

The woman of my dreams was within reach and yet so far gone that I knew she could not be mine, even if she did regain her memories. I would forever be left wanting.

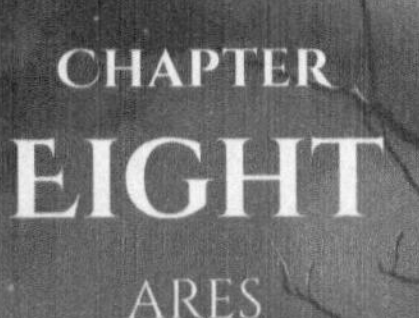

CHAPTER

EIGHT

ARES

Leaving her side again after such a short and bittersweet reunion was extremely difficult. If it were for any other reason, I would have stayed, grabbed her in my arms and never let go. She looked exactly the same, but without her memories she wasn't the same woman. I could tell that she had the strongest connection to me still, but even after making amends with Achilles and letting myself love my half-brother again, I didn't want to leave her with him.

"The sooner we get this over with, the sooner you can be back in her arms," Victor said from my side.

I turned and smiled at him. "I know. I just—"

"Don't like leaving her with your half-brother, especially since you can tell she has some of her memories? Achilles is the most moral Sidhe I know and he won't make any advances on her while you are out risking your life. Besides, what you're doing isn't just for her to regain her memories. She is the key to everything."

"I don't think Achilles will try anything either, but…what

if she starts remembering and I'm not there? What if she only remembers him and not me?"

Victor rolled his eyes. "You two dreamed again, right?"

"Don't patronize me, Victor. I know that we are still connected, but I have no way of knowing what Hera did to Artemis. If the dragons aren't as powerful as we think, she could end up dying." I wouldn't let that happen. I refused to let her die now that I'd found her.

"Let's just focus on getting to Rhea's Temple," he said softly.

We increased our speed and made it to the City of Rhea, which was the gatekeeper to the Temple, faster than I'd thought we would. Even during the human reign this had been left untouched. Of course, since it was in the Himalayas and freezing cold, I wasn't surprised that even after the uprising, Maurice had left it alone as well. Rhea was the strongest being on the planet and I for one would not want to be on her bad side.

"It's more deserted than I thought it would be," Victor said with a frown.

I looked over and saw his fangs fully extended, which was something he only did when scaring someone or when he couldn't retract them due to his overwhelming thirst.

"I told you to eat on the way here. You'll just have to settle for a rabbit to quench the fire for now."

Victor grumbled, and we started through the empty town. The buildings looked freshly made, but they had to have been at least a thousand years old judging by the architecture. The wolf side of me felt uneasy about walking into someone else's den, but this was for Artemis so I would just have to deal with the feeling.

Victor disappeared a moment and then reappeared with

two rabbits. He drained the blood from them and then tossed them to me. "You need to eat too, in case Mother asks a price from you."

I ate the meat from the skinny rabbits and snapped off one of the rabbit's feet. I held it out to Victor. "Want a good luck charm?"

He swatted the foot away when I waved it at him and he shook his head in disgust. "I never understood why the humans used to believe that. And it was rather disgusting that they kept the piece of animal on their key chains of all places." I smiled and then Victor sighed. "I do miss the human world though. I miss the restaurants, the movies and most of all the women who threw themselves at me because they wanted to please me and were attracted to me and thought it was exotic to be with a vampire."

"You mean women don't throw themselves at your feet now?"

Victor groaned. "Yes, they do, but only because I'm the big bad vampire prince. I'm not my father, Ares, you know that. I don't like to be feared." I arched my eyebrow and Victor smiled. "Okay, I like to be feared a little, but not all the time and definitely not from the women I want to bed."

A loud growling brought my attention to the skies above us. The moon was gone and I couldn't see, but I definitely felt like I was being watched. "What is it, Victor? I'm blind here." I caught the dim shape of something flying through the air above us, but I couldn't make out the form.

"It looks like a griffin," he said with a bit of awe.

I started running and yelled, "Race you to the door!"

Victor caught up to me easily as the griffins began diving at me and pulling at my hair. Their claws raked my chest and back, drawing blood.

"I get the wolf. You can have the leech," said a deep and growly voice.

"No, he's a halfbreed and we agreed that I'd get the next halfbreed that came through," argued a second voice.

I was beginning to worry when a commanding voice so beautiful and melodic that it made me stop running and stand still, yelled, "None shall touch him! He has a golden aura!"

Ahead of us was the temple steps and standing in the doorway was a woman more beautiful than any other I had seen. She had hair the color of wheat and eyes of emeralds. She was so powerful that I dropped to my knees instantly and bowed my head. "Mother," I whimpered.

She floated down the steps of the temple and knelt in front of me. She touched my face and frowned in concern. "You are in pain. What do you need from me, halfbreed son?"

She was right, I was in pain. Pain at having been separated from the woman I loved. Pain at not knowing for sure if she was alive or dead. Pain at not knowing if she'd been with another man in the past one hundred years. Pain at my love not knowing me.

"I need your consent to continue being with my mate. It is the price the dragons asked in order to assist me in recovering the memories which were stolen from her." I could barely whisper with her so close to me. She was the true Mother of us all, the Mother of even Asena.

"You love her more than anyone else. You have not touched another woman even though you have been separated for over one hundred years. I have not met a man so devoted as you and with a perfect golden aura in many years."

"Golden aura?" I asked.

She smiled. "When a man is pure of heart, void of evil and

knows the love of a perfect match, his aura will glow golden. I will give you my consent…"

I looked up at her and smiled.

"…but you must defeat my champion," she finished.

"Your champion?" Victor asked.

Rhea turned to Victor and laid her hand against his cheek. "Oh, son of the Darkness. You are powerful, but not powerful enough. I think I shall grant you a gift as well if this task is completed. Yes, yes, I will give you more power if you and the halfbreed can defeat my champion."

"Who is your champion?" I finally managed to ask.

She wagged her finger at me. "You must agree or decline first."

"I agree. I will do anything to have my mate back," I answered without any more hesitation. I really hoped her champion wasn't that great of a fighter.

She threw her head back and laughed maniacally.

I looked at Victor, but he only shrugged. Women were weird, apparently from the beginning of time.

Rhea looked back at me. "I do not expect you to be able to kill my champion since I would not have picked a weak being for such an honor, but I do expect you or your vampire friend to be able to draw blood. If one drop of blood is drawn from him, then you will have what you ask for and your vampire friend will have more power than any other in the world. You agree?"

Victor and I nodded. I stood and brushed myself off. This was my chance. The one thing I had to do to get Artemis back. I would not fail.

The temple doors flew open, and I watched in awe as a tall man with thick cords of muscle and a perfect physique walked down the steps. His eyes were the purest blue I'd seen, even purer than my own. He stopped beside Rhea and asked, "You summoned me?"

Rhea hugged the man and whispered, "They need only draw a drop of blood from you. Fight well, Hyperion. Do not disappoint me."

Hyperion? Oh gods.

He stood, and I knew it had to be true. The father of the moon, stars and the sun. The father of all preternaturals.

"Oh, crap," Victor said softly.

I ripped my pants off, took a half-shift and then launched myself at Hyperion just as Victor charged at him, too. Hyperion smiled, rolled his shoulders in a circle and said, "It's been so long since I've had a challenge."

I jumped in the air as I dodged Blu's tail and then shot him in the back with fire. I blocked an attack from Theseus behind me, smiling at my quick reflexes. I grabbed onto Theseus' arm, tossed him over my shoulder and dropped onto his fallen body, delivering blow after blow to his face and body.

"Enough!" Blu roared behind me. I stood up off of Theseus and prepared to attack Blu, but he pinned me to the ground with his foot and growled at me. "I understand that you are worried about the princes, but you are taking it out on Theseus' body."

I hated being pinned. As a wolf I hated being trapped. my body began to glow in the reflection of Blu's eye. He grabbed me and then tossed me into the air. I pulled my wings from my back and flapped them furiously to keep from flying any farther away. I started to fly back towards Blu, but something slammed into my side and sent me careening sideways with my wings pinned against my body. I struggled against what held me until I looked up and realized it was Theseus.

He let us fall to the ground and then pinned me on my back to the ground. "I command you to stop."

I growled at him and bared my teeth. "Get off of me. You do not command me."

"Are you going to behave?" he asked in a reasonable and irritating tone.

I struggled against his hold, but then he used his power to make a shield and slammed it against me. I gasped and then anger overrode my other senses. I used my wings to push us up off of the ground and changed my hand into a paw to stab him in the stomach, but suddenly I was paralyzed.

"You are going to hurt someone you do not wish to harm if you don't control yourself, Hatchling," said the Council.

"I can't just sit here while he's out on such a dangerous mission! I can hardly sleep and I need to do something!" I yelled. I had never before yelled at a dragon, much less the Council and I expected a punishment, but at that moment I didn't care. The shirt the werewolf prince had given me had lost his scent quickly and I knew it was my own fault for smelling it and touching it so much.

"Very well, we will teach you a technique which will consume you, body and mind, until you have learned it. We warn you, it will not be easy to master and may destroy you if you are not powerful enough."

"Please. I need to do something," I said in a much quieter voice. I knew it was an honor for the dragons to teach anyone and that I should feel humbled, but the churning in my stomach at the thought of losing the prince was too much.

"Go wash, eat and then return to us with an open mind and quiet heart," said the Council.

I bowed to them and hurried to do as they asked. I washed my hair and body, ate some meat and bread and then sat in the center of my tent with my legs crossed as I meditated. Normally a request that I have a quiet heart was easy, but since meeting the man who claimed to be my mate and who I had an undeniable bond with, I couldn't. I closed my eyes and relaxed my body in sections. Once my body was relaxed, I focused on the inner turmoil consuming me and slowly released it.

The truth about who I was would be revealed once the prince comes back. The prince will return safely because he swore he would and because he is one of the most powerful beings on the earth.

Continuing in this fashion I released all of my worries and quieted my heart. Feeling better than I had in weeks, I walked out of my tent and to the waiting Council.

I bowed down before them and whispered, "I apologize for my discourteous behavior earlier. Please forgive my insolent actions and words."

"You are forgiven, Hatchling. Are you ready to learn what we are offering to teach you?"

I stood and bowed my head. "Yes. I am."

Blu stood off to the right, watching and waiting. I knew he wasn't just curious about what they were going to teach me, but he was also there to protect me if something happened.

The Council began humming and singing and then disappeared. I stared at the empty spot where five large dragons had just occupied. The humming returned behind me. I whipped around and found the Council now behind me. *Translocation.*

I moaned in pain as a memory of a beautiful woman transporting me from a fight to a strange town flashed across my eyes. I opened my eyes and found that I'd dropped to my knees and Blu was humming with his nose against my head as he tried to heal the pain.

"What did you see?" asked the Council.

"A woman, I believe Sidhe, though at the time I didn't know that. She teleported me from a fight with vampires to a town in the woods. There are periods of pain in between and I don't seem to have memories for those brief lapses, but..." I screamed again as I understood that she was the woman who had stolen my memories.

"Good, Hatchling. Now we know who the woman is that stole your memories. She is a very powerful Sidhe and it will not be easy to break the barrier she placed."

"Barrier? You mean I still have my memories? She didn't steal them away?"

The Council looked at me in confusion. "Why do you believe they were stolen?"

I groaned. The pain in my head returned as I recalled specifics of the memory. "I remember that the images slipped out of my head, like mud slipping through my fingers. It was as though she plucked them from my head."

The Council went completely silent as they communicated to each other. It was rare that the Council was silent for such a long period of time and it made me very nervous. Finally, they said, "We will not discuss this further until the wolf prince has returned. Now, let us teach you how to teleport yourself and others."

I stood up and patted Blu's nose reassuringly. "Okay."

CHAPTER

TEN

ARES

My body hadn't ached so badly and in so many places at once in hundreds of years. Covered in sweat and panting like a child, I felt pathetic and weak. I looked over and found Victor in the same state, except his fangs were bared to their longest, reaching down past his lower lip. It was a situation neither of us had been in for a very long time. How could one individual be so powerful?

"We need to change our tactics," said Victor from beside me.

Hyperion was sweating slightly, but our two minute breaks completely revived him whereas we were still winded and still in pain.

"Obviously, but what do you suggest?" I asked with a growl. We'd been fighting for an hour and forty minutes and even with our combined attacks, Victor and I couldn't even scratch him.

"I don't know yet. I was hoping you might have an idea. You are the God of War."

I glared at him. "I'm the God of War against humans and

other races, not the Father of Preternaturals!"

Hyperion charged at us, and I ducked just in time. I turned and slashed at his exposed back, but his fist smashed into my face as he spun around in a whirlwind. I crashed to the stone floor and snarled. This was not working.

Victor punched at Hyperion from the front, so I ran and jumped, trying to hop onto his back, but his foot rose without his head even turning and he kicked me backwards while he punched Victor in the chest.

"Do you have eyes in the back of your head?" I asked as frustration gripped me.

Hyperion laughed. "You know as well as I that your other senses can help you know when someone is approaching from the back. Your breathing is as loud as a baby rhinoceros."

I growled at him and attacked from the front, punching and slashing at his arms. No matter how fast I moved, my claws never reached his skin.

Rhea watched with glowing eyes from a throne the griffins had brought out of the temple for her to sit.

Victor rolled his neck and shoulders and said, "We need to use a cheap tactic."

I turned and stared at him. "You're serious?"

He smiled. "Do you really care if we win legitimately or not?"

Hyperion growled. "Are you two weaklings going to stand there and whine all day or are we going to fight? If you want to surrender, I'm fine with that, too."

"I will never surrender!" I yelled. I had to win. *I have to do this for Artemis.* I counted down from five and then charged Hyperion. His dagger pierced the side of my stomach just as Victor stabbed at Hyperion's other side. Without even turning, Hyperion swatted Victor, catching him in the side and sending him flying. Victor landed on his feet and skidded at least fifteen feet back. I pulled away from Hyperion and growled as I put a hand over my wound.

Victor hissed furiously and I saw his power release around him in a thick black cloud. "Ready?" he yelled at me as he disappeared.

I called upon the power of the moon, which hangs above us in her ever-present beauty, and charged forward. I exchanged blows with Hyperion and as my strength was waning shouted, "Now!"

Victor's body materialized from my shadow and he slid underneath my legs, between Hyperion's, and grabbed Hyperion around the arms.

I squatted down and slashed his leg, opening a small cut.

Hyperion yelled, broke free from Victor's grasp and picked me up by the throat. "No! I refuse to be defeated by a halfbreed!"

"You have been defeated, Hyperion. Release your grandson," said Rhea softly.

Hyperion looked as though he wanted to object, but after one look at Rhea's serious face, he dropped me to the ground and stepped back. "I admit defeat."

If only they would assist us in righting the balance of the world and killing Maurice, we could win the battle quickly and easily. I understood their desire to remain neutral, but it would make things so much easier.

Victor limped over to me and said, "That was easier than I thought it would be."

I forced back the smile which tried to surface and turned towards Rhea as I still clutched my bleeding side. "We have completed your task. Will you give me your blessing as you agreed?"

Rhea placed her hand on my forehead and said, "I, Mother Rhea, give you, Ares Lupine of the Werewolves and Sidhe, my blessing to continue as a mated pair with Artemis Lupine. May the dragons restore her memories and bring back the woman you love."

It felt like a weight had been lifted from my shoulders, yet I sagged to the ground and felt tears on my face. I'd done it. I'd completed the task and now Artemis was finally going to get her memories back!

"You, Victor of the Vampires, have shown great loyalty to your friend despite the differences in your races. Therefore, I pronounce you as Ruler of the Children of the Night and give you the power to hold that title. May your reign be brighter than your father's." Rhea's hands began to glow and she placed them on either side of Victor's head. He moaned in pleasure and then his body glowed with an eerie black light. It was like seeing a Sidhe glowing white, but his light was like the night instead of the stars.

Victor turned to me with flames flickering in the back of his black eyes. I smiled at him and asked, "Are you glad you came with me now?"

Victor laughed and reined in the power he'd been given. "That is a definite rush. I'm looking forward to using it against my father."

Rhea kissed each of us on the forehead and whispered to me, "Run home. She is close to breaking."

I blinked at her for a moment until the words made sense. Then I turned and ran without another thought. *Artemis.*

Victor caught up to me and asked, "What is it?"

"Artemis," I whispered, knowing he wouldn't need any more of an explanation.

ELEVEN

CHANDRA

I'd been training for an hour straight and had only managed to teleport two feet. The Council assured me that with more practice I'd be able to move farther. I closed my eyes and pictured the place I wanted to move to, the top of Blu's head ten feet away from me. Power built inside me, followed by pain, then nausea and then I was falling. My eyes snapped open and I straightened as I stood on top of Blu's head. "Yes!" I yelled victoriously. Blu huffed in mock irritation as I stood upon his head, but I could tell he was pleased.

I dropped to the ground, but just as I was landing pain erupted in my head. It felt like a crack had opened in something that encased my power and allowed it to leak out. The pain was more intense than anything I'd felt before and I couldn't even scream. I landed on my side, smacking my head against the ground, but didn't feel the additional pain.

Blu pressed his nose to my head and tried to help me, but the pain was beyond even his repair.

"Step back, Draco-Blu. She cannot be helped except by the two tied to her," said the Council.

On cue, the Sidhe prince dropped to the ground beside me with a grimace of pain on his face. "It's going to be alright. He's on his way and will be here soon."

Another man dropped to my side and placed his hands on me. I inhaled his scent and screamed in pain as a memory of him holding me while we both wept played across my open eyelids. Black dots began to cover my vision and I screamed again as my head throbbed in pain.

"Help us, please," the Sidhe prince begged the Council.

"Please, darlin', just relax. He's almost here. Just hold on for a few more minutes," said the man with a slightly southern accent.

My body began to twitch as the wolf side of me tried to find a way to save us. I growled and held my body together. "I...will...not...change."

Wind stirred above me and then the wolf prince dropped to the ground beside me. He tilted my face so I could look into his eyes. "Stay with me. I'm here now. Hold on." He turned away from me and said, "I have gained permission from Rhea. Please, help us now."

The Council said, "In order to restore her memories and give her full access to her power, you must divulge her full true name to her as well as both of the names of the princes she is tied to. Once you do that, her power will release, her memories will return and we will help you control her mind and body so that she does not become too overwhelmed."

"I understand," whispered the wolf prince.

"Me too," whispered the Sidhe prince.

"Begin," said the Council.

"You are Artemis Lupine, daughter of Darren of the Were-wolves and Athena of the Sidhe, *passt genau* of Ares and bound to Achilles. You are princess of both the Sidhe and werewolf realms," said the princes together.

My head throbbed excruciatingly and black spots danced across my vision.

"I am Ares Lupine, prince of the werewolves and descendant of Beatrice of the Werewolves and Zeus of the Sidhe and your *passt genau*," said the wolf prince. My vision blackened completely and my body arched up off the ground as my power released.

"I am Achilles, prince of the Sidhe and rightful heir to the throne, descendant of Hera and Zeus of the Sidhe and your bound match," said the Sidhe prince.

Everything disappeared in a world of white and black. I knew I was screaming, but I couldn't hear anything besides the frantic pounding of my heart. Visions of Ares meeting me, fighting for me, making love to me replayed. Visions of Achilles fighting beside me, flying with me, teaching me to open my wings and telling me he loved me replayed. I saw my father. My mother. Koda. Matt. Maurice and his vampires fighting us. Hera taking me and stealing my memories.

The Council, Blu and every dragon in the Lair began singing as they tried to help me. There was so much magic in one place that it made me afraid of the possible repercussions.

I had no voice left for screaming and the power within me felt like it was going to rip me apart. Suddenly every memory I'd ever had fell into place.

"Ares. Achilles. Koda." I whispered their names.

The dragons sang louder than I'd ever heard before. Ares, Achilles, Koda and Theseus all touched me as they used their powers to help.

"I am Artemis Lupine!" I screamed. The pressure and

power within me exploded outwards and left me feeling weightless. Every being screamed around me as my power was unleashed upon them.

CHAPTER

TWELVE

ARTEMIS

The magic and dust settled and I could breathe again. It seemed like a millennium since I had last opened my eyes, but when I did the joy was better than anything I'd ever felt before. Kneeling one foot away from me was the man who had loved me since discovering me in a small human town. The man who had been so patient with me while I learned about who I really was. The man who would protect me at any cost. His black hair was shaggier than the last time I'd seen him, but his blue eyes sparkled brighter than ever as he looked at me. I could see the hope and worry in his eyes.

How could he have survived the past one hundred years without me by his side? I doubted that I could have held myself together if I hadn't been able to locate him in one hundred years.

I felt my connection to Achilles, but nothing compared with the fierce pull, staggering desire, and love I felt for Ares. We both stood up off of the ground, and I walked slowly towards him. He stood perfectly still as he watched me approach him, but I could see the slight tremor in his arms.

He was such a magnificent man, and he was all mine, had always been mine, and would always be mine. I wanted to jump into his arms and roll on him to cover myself in his scent, but this was not the place for that.

I stopped in front of him as my body quivered and said, *"Verus amor vincit omnia.* True love conquers all, even one hundred years of separation and a woman's plot to erase you from my memories."

He shuddered, and I wrapped my arms around his neck, kissing him fiercely. His arms were instantly around me in an almost painful embrace, but I didn't care. I was in his arms and we were together again. The kiss was intense yet tender. I felt like I could conquer worlds when he kissed me like that.

He pulled back first and stared into my eyes with tears in his. "Artemis, I've missed you," he whispered.

I buried my nose into his neck and inhaled his delicious scent. "Ares," I sighed. It felt so good to say his name.

Someone cleared their throat and I pulled back to find Achilles and Koda looking at me expectantly. It was almost painful as I tried to decide who to hug first, but Achilles won. I hugged him tightly to me and kissed his lips as his thoughts flooded my mind. *I've missed you so much. It's been so hard not knowing where you were. Or what condition you were in.*

I pulled back from him and smiled. "Thank you. I am truly sorry that I can't say the same. If I had had my memories, I would."

Koda pulled me from Achilles and wrapped me in one of his famous bear hugs. "I've been worried sick about you."

I laughed and relaxed in his hold. "I'm sorry."

Theseus stood back from our group and I remembered his worried words to me before we'd arrived. I walked to him and hugged him. "Thank you for keeping me safe and sane between the times I was able to see Ares. I have not forgotten you, my friend."

Theseus exhaled in relief and hugged me tightly. "Thank you."

Koda groaned behind me. "Great, now my son is taking her attention away from me. I'll never win."

I pulled back from Theseus and looked from Koda to him and back. "He's your father?" Theseus nodded. I laughed. "No wonder you looked familiar to me!"

I pulled away from Theseus and walked into Ares' arms. Ares turned my face up to his and whispered, "I love you, Artemis."

My lips pulled up into a smile, and I wrapped my arms around him. "I love you too, Ares."

He sighed loudly. "It has been too long since I last heard those words." His lips were pressed to mine before I could say anything else.

I pulled back from him and stood between him and Achilles so that each could hold my hand. Their powers began to flow between me and I could feel the wound Ares neglected to inform us about. I placed my hand on his side, and he grunted in pleasure and pain as the wound knitted itself together.

I looked up at the Council standing near us and said, "Thank you, dragons. I am in your debt." I pulled away from Ares and Achilles and walked to the center to turn and look at each dragon. "I will always remember the great honor that you have given me."

The Council bowed their heads to me. "We will always remember you, Hatchling. It has been an honor to keep you safe over the years."

I turned to Blu and bowed until my forehead touched the

ground. "Draco-Blu, you have been my greatest friend and guardian. I am forever in your debt."

Blu dropped his head into a bow. "There is no debt to be paid, Artemis. Just remember who your allies are and never forget the kindness of a dragon."

I held up the dragon scale which was secured on a string around my neck. "I will always remember you, my friend."

Blu wrapped his head around me and hummed against my body. "I will miss you."

Tears sprang to my eyes and I latched on to his neck. "I will miss you as well. Tell Fira goodbye for me."

Blu hummed louder and then pulled away. Ares and Achilles each grabbed one of my hands and I exhaled in relief as their touch eased the ache in my body.

I turned from them to find Victor, who was standing off to the side smiling at us. I walked to him and hugged him tightly. "Thank you for everything you have done, Victor."

Victor hugged me back and kissed my cheek lightly. "I am glad to see you whole and safe *Mon papillon*."

I pulled back and wiped at the tears under his eyes. "I thought vampires weren't supposed to cry?"

He smiled and whispered, "It had been so long that I dreaded we would not find you. I am just…often in my experience these types of things end badly and I feared the worst might be true when we finally did find you."

I laughed. "Victor, you know me. I never get into trouble."

That received a round of laughter from all of the men gathered. I looked at Victor curiously a moment and then asked, "When did you gain so much power?"

Victor's tears forgotten, he smiled arrogantly, "Rhea gifted me for assisting Ares."

I looked at the lighter tint to his aura and asked, "Did she make you more human? Your aura is less black."

Victor shrugged. "I feel more like a vampire than I ever have before. I don't question what was done, just enjoy the powers that I've been granted."

Ares pulled me into his arms again and nuzzled my hair with his nose as he inhaled long draughts of my scent.

"Where are we going now?" I asked.

"We are going to prepare for the war," answered Victor.

I groaned. "You know, I'd hoped you would have taken care of that, not let the world fall into darkness as it has." I pulled out of Ares' arms and asked, "And what is going on with all of the halfbreed kidnappings? I was scared out of my mind these past sixty or so years that I've been with Selene."

Ares sighed. "We have much to catch you up on. I'd prefer if we could make it at least to our base camp before we discussed it though."

Base camp? Since when had they started talking like military men?

Victor changed into a bat and screeched at us as he took off into the sky towards the Lair's exit. I turned and bowed to the Council one more time and then let my wings out from my back. Achilles and Theseus let out their wings and then Achilles picked up Ares and Theseus picked up Koda.

I giggled as I joined them in the air and said, "Koda that is so cute that your son can carry you!"

Koda stuck his tongue out at me. "I may be happy that you're back, but I will still kick your butt."

I rolled my eyes. "You couldn't take me even before I gained more power."

Every eye, including Victor's bat ones, turned to me. Achilles asked, "Gained more power? What do you mean?"

I waved at them dismissively. "I'll show you when we get to your 'base camp'."

The men grumbled their agreements, and we flew out of the Lair and out into the night. I reveled in my ability to fly again and somersaulted and spun in the air in a crazy dance of freedom.

"Been a while since you've last flown, Artemis?" asked Achilles.

I giggled happily. "Much too long. I was pretending to be human so I couldn't risk outing myself just to enjoy some flight time. I'd forgotten how wonderful the wind feels under my wings." I flipped onto my back and dove down and then back up again.

Theseus and Koda were discussing something with serious looks on their faces so I flew over to be nosy. "What's up?"

Koda asked, "Did you recognize the Sidhe who brought the vampires to attack you?"

I frowned. "He seemed familiar, like we were connected somehow, but I don't think I've ever seen his face before." I scoured my regained memories and shook my head. "No, I've never met him before. Why? Do you know him?"

Koda exhaled. "I might. We'll discuss it further at camp."

I flew over to Achilles and Ares and stayed by their sides the rest of the way.

"Where are we?" I asked as we dropped onto a beach where a large stone house sat alone.

"Ireland," answered Ares.

I grabbed Ares' hand and then Achilles'. Ares called, "Come out."

Over a hundred men and women walked out of the house to stand before us on the beach. All eyes trained on me and my instant reaction was to cower, but then I remembered who I was and straightened my spine, meeting all of their eyes. I expected some people to avert their gazes or meet mine defiantly. I did not expect them to all drop to one knee and bow their heads.

THIRTEEN

I looked at Ares and Achilles. "What's going on?"

Ares and Achilles stepped away from me and walked towards the group. Achilles said, "We all knew this day was going to come. You've all been training hard and so, tonight we celebrate."

Ares took over. "We will celebrate the return of my mate. We will celebrate the return of the prophesied one. We will celebrate our impending victory."

The group cheered, but continued to keep their heads bowed in submission. *What the hell is going on?*

Ares turned to me. "We found a way to create an army to combat the vampires. An army which is stronger, more powerful and has fewer weaknesses."

Achilles said, "We have been training them hard in preparation for your return. I hope they are to your liking."

"What the hell are you talking about?" I asked. "What are they? Who are they? What do you mean you created them?" I looked from Ares to Achilles and then at the group.

Theseus stood up from amongst the group and said, "We

are mixed breeds, like you, though not nearly as powerful as you, Princess."

"Mixed breeds?" I walked to the group and inhaled their scents. "Oh, wow. Whoa." They were all half wolf and half Sidhe. "How did you create them?"

Ares smirked. "You see, Artemis. When a man and woman lie together…"

I stared at him in horror. "They're your…" I couldn't finish the sentence. I knew that I was gone a long time, but this was too much for me. I turned away from Ares and started walking down the beach, but Victor stepped into my path and shook his head with a smile on his lips. "You misunderstand, *mon papillon*. These are not Ares and Achilles' children."

I blinked at him. "But he just said…"

Victor silenced me with a glare. "Would I lie to you?"

A smile teased the corner of my lips. "You want me to answer that honestly?"

Victor laughed. "I am being truthful, Artemis. Neither of your mates has broken his vow to you."

I frowned at him as I looked back at Ares and Achilles talking quietly to each other. "I've never mated with Achilles, Victor. You know that."

He shrugged. "You are still bound to him as you are to Ares. It is not so different."

I rolled my eyes. "Not the point. So, if he didn't create them, then who did?"

Victor said, "Koda, among others from the pack who are on Ares' side."

"I'm sure that was a difficult task for them," I muttered. I felt like an idiot for storming away from Ares and Achilles.

Ares walked up to me and asked, "What's wrong?"

I buried my face in his neck and whispered, "I thought they were your children."

Ares pushed me back and held me at arm's length. "Artemis, you should know me better than that."

I blushed and said, "I was gone over a hundred years. I didn't know…"

Ares asked, "What about you? I won't be angry since you didn't have your memories, but…"

"No!" I yelled a little too loudly. I lowered my voice, "No, I didn't. I lived in the witches' coven surrounded only by women. Oh and Draco-Blu, but no, I didn't."

Ares hugged me again and kissed my cheek. "I still can't believe you're here after so long."

I laid my head on his shoulder and sighed. "It does feel like it has been an awfully long time since we've been together."

"Yes, well, could we finish with the introductions?" Achilles asked with a hint of anger in his voice.

"I'm still curious to see what Artemis meant about gaining power," Victor said behind us.

Ares walked with me back to the bowing group. "You just need to accept them as your followers and we can move on."

"Um, okay. I accept you as my followers," I said nervously.

The group stood up and then returned to the house. How could all of them fit in there?

"Alright, show us this new power," said Victor.

I looked around. "Are there any vampires who could be hurt by the sun here?" Victor shook his head. I lifted my hands up in front of my chest, palms facing each other. Warmth filled my body as I called upon my magic, which was much easier now that I was whole, and a ball of sun formed between my hands. I looked up and found Victor, Ares, Koda and Achilles staring at me in complete shock. "Sunlight," I said.

All of the men walked up to me and examined the orb of sunlight I held.

"Incredible," whispered Ares.

"I didn't know any of us could do this anymore," said Achilles.

"How big can you make it?" asked Victor.

Theseus said, "She sent it out in an expanding ring to turn a group of vampires who had surrounded us into ash."

Victor's eyes widened. "Show me."

I shrugged and released the orb and then formed a ring of sunlight around my body. I gathered my magic and then sent the ring out, expanding it as it moved farther away from my body. Instead of letting it go as I'd done previously though, I held it when it was about a mile in circumference.

"Remarkable," said Victor. "No wonder my father renewed his quest for her. Who did you do this in front of?"

I looked at Koda. "The guy you were asking me about. I did it in front of him."

Koda's eyes widened. "Oh no." He turned to Ares. "I think she met Apollo."

Everyone went still at the mention of his name. "Who's Apollo?" I asked softly.

Ares shook his head. "We don't have time to talk about him. We need to get everyone together and move. If it was Apollo, he'll be searching for her."

"Ares! Why are you still keeping me in the dark?"

Ares sighed. "He's the leader of a faction of vampires, which are stronger than the normal ones. Apollo is taking beings like trolls and Sidhe and turning them into vampires. He alone controls the group."

Vampire-Sidhe? Unbelievable.

Ares picked up my hand and smiled. "Come on, let's hunt first."

Koda shifted forms, shredding his clothes and then pranced along the beach as he waited for us. Theseus, Achilles and Victor walked to the house while I stripped. Ares watched me and I felt the blush on my cheeks before I realized I was embarrassed. I shifted forms and stretched. *Ah. It feels good to be a wolf again.*

Ares licked my muzzle, now in his wolf form. *Ready?*

Koda yipped and ran up the beach towards the distant trees. I chased after Koda and Ares ran at my side. I caught up to Koda and nipped his flank playfully. *Too slow.* I sped past him with Ares right on my heels.

Koda dove under my legs, making me tumble head over tail and then Ares was on top of me. We nipped and played for what felt like hours before collapsing into a pile together. Ares and Koda shifted positions until I was lying between, their heads and tails forming a circle around me. Finally, I was back with my pack. After so many years as a lone wolf I couldn't imagine a better place to be.

After our pack nap, we returned to the house which I thought would be filled to capacity, but it was strangely open. "Where is everyone?" I asked.

Achilles pointed down. "Underground. We built a lower level down there to accommodate the large number of our pack."

Victor asked, "Where did you learn that new sunlight power, Artemis? Did the witches teach you that?"

I shook my head. "A vampire attacked me one night while I was walking back to the coven. I just kept thinking how the fight would be a lot easier if I could use sunlight instead of fire and then, boom, sunlight burst out of my hand and poof went the vampire. It took a while, but Selene managed to create a spell which lets her do a similar thing."

Victor tapped his chin thoughtfully. "It might be beneficial to us if we contacted the witches and asked for their alliance in the upcoming battle."

Ares nodded. "I was thinking the same thing. I wanted to stop and talk to Selene anyways and thank her for protecting Artemis all these years."

I looked at the amount of space between Ares, Achilles and I. Why were they now staying apart from me?

Achilles looked at me, and I remembered he could hear my thoughts. He smiled and walked to me, taking my hand. "It was nothing intentional, we just didn't want to overwhelm you or cause problems."

I felt a piece of me calm and looked at Ares. "Are you still bothered by this? When I left, you two weren't really on the best of terms."

Ares smiled. "We have worked out our issues."

Somehow, I didn't think they had resolved the one major issue we had between the three of us while I was gone.

I walked to the living room which was sparsely furnished and sat in a rocking chair facing the rest of the couches. "Now, how about you all fill me in on the last one hundred and five years?"

The men all took seats facing me and looked at each other for several minutes before Koda began. "When Hera stole you, things went a little crazy. Ares and Darren were fighting, but when you got teleported to such a far distance, Ares strength sapped and Darren got in a few good shots. More vampires poured in and with both Ares and Achilles distracted, we knew we wouldn't win. So, we ran."

My mouth gaped open. "You ran away?"

Koda frowned. "Yep. We turned tail and ran. We escaped to Lyngvi, but when we got there Darius had us thrown in jail for some fake charges. He knew he couldn't have us murdered, but not even mom could get us out. So, we were all stuck in jail for fifty years."

"That's a pretty harsh punishment for fake charges."

Koda shrugged. "Fifty years isn't as long as it is to humans."

"How'd you get out of jail?" I asked.

Achilles said, "Hera."

I turned to him. "Hera got you out?"

He nodded. "She popped into our cells and took us to her Court."

"Why would she help you when she was the one who repressed my memories?" I asked with a bit of an angry tone.

"Because I never intended to keep you separated for so long," said a familiar female voice.

I spun around and before I'd even thought it, my wings were out, my skin glowed, and my hands became covered in flames. Every eye was focused on me as I floated above the ground and glared at the woman who had caused me so much pain and separated me from my pack and myself for so long. "What are you doing here?" I asked in a voice that boomed with power.

Victor circled me slowly while Ares and Achilles moved closer. "She really has grown in power. I thought she only meant that she had learned a new spell, but this...this is incredible."

Hera kept her gaze level with mine, but for the first time, I saw fear in her eyes. "Artemis, please let me explain."

Anger boiled inside me and in a millisecond, I moved across the room and had Hera up against the wall by her throat. "Give me one good reason why I shouldn't rip your head off right here and now."

"I only did it to save Achilles. Please, you must understand what lengths a mother would go to save her child."

"I know nothing of a mother's love!" I shouted at her. "Or have you forgotten that I was supposed to be killed when I was born?"

Ares and Achilles each touched one of my arms.

"Calm down, please," whispered Achilles.

Ares whispered, "We believe Hera and have forgiven her. Please, let her go."

My primitive side screamed for vengeance, but I subdued it and released her and my powers. "Fine, but if you so much as give me a cross look, I'll kill you."

Hera started to open her mouth and then thought better of it. "You're more a queen now than you were before."

I turned away from her and stomped to the other side of the room. "Why were you helping Maurice?"

"At the time, I thought he was the most powerful and couldn't afford to lose my people in a fight against him. Had I known that you were indeed the prophesied one, I would have never agreed to assist him. But I didn't follow his instructions exactly. You see, he wanted me to kill you, but due to Achilles binding you two together, that would mean killing my own son. I wiped your memory and sent you away from him so you would be out of Maurice's view and thus, safe. I did the only thing that could keep you both alive."

"Alive, but terrified," I whispered to the fireplace mantle in front of me.

"I am sorry, Artemis. If I could find a way to make up for what I'd done, I would," she whispered.

I turned back to Ares. "So, while you were locked up, Maurice took over the human world?"

He nodded. "He completed the take over and instead of being equal with the other races, the vampires ruled and he took over as king."

"And then the reign of terror began." I looked at Koda. "Why were halfbreeds being kidnapped?"

"The vampires kidnapped some in an attempt to find you and to build their army, but we also went to the already living halfbreeds we could find and asked them to join our pack. Each that we asked came willingly."

I paced along the living room floor. "What's our plan? How does this Apollo guy figure into it?" Hera's body stilled and it looked like she wasn't even breathing. I walked towards her. "Who's Apollo?"

She swallowed and then her queen face was back on. "No one of consequence."

Before I could say anything, she disappeared. I growled and punched the wall, which buckled under my fist. "Why does everyone always hide things from me?!"

A man that looked to be in his late teens ran into the house. "Ares!"

Ares rushed to him. "What is it?"

The man caught his breath and then noticed me. "Oh. Wow."

I frowned at him and he started to move towards me, but Ares growled at him. "Speak!"

The man shook his head as though clearing it. "There's a group of vampire hybrids coming this way. That guy is leading them."

I rummaged through my bag until I found an open backed shirt which Selene made specifically for me to wear while my wings were out. All of the men looked at me questioningly as I stripped out of my current shirt, which was ripped since releasing my wings, and put on the new one. I shimmied out of my pants and put on a pair of short shorts and then put my fists touching in front of me. "By the power of the stars, grant me a weapon to fight this foe." I pulled my hands apart and a sword of light appeared between them.

"Who taught you that?" asked Achilles as his eyes went wide.

I shrugged. "I dreamed the words and when I tried them the next morning, it worked." I traced the outline of one of the vines on my face and whispered, "May the stars and moon aid me in my battle for peace." My power as well as the power of the moon and stars made my body glow bright and my vines surged. I smiled at Ares. "See you outside." I ran from the house and onto the beach where I could just make out the group coming my way.

Ares appeared at my side. "Artemis, please. Just wait in the house."

I laughed. "That didn't work before and it's definitely not going to work now."

Ares sighed. "Fine, but please, stay beside me."

I kissed his lips and whispered, "Yes, Alpha."

Ares kissed me a little bit longer, nipping my bottom lip at the end which made me growl in frustration. "Just think of that as incentive to stay alive for the private celebration afterwards."

The rest of our group and pack joined us, standing behind Ares and me. The man Koda referred to as Apollo stopped across the beach from us with his vampire hybrids fanned out behind him. "Surrender the girl and we will leave the rest of you alone."

Ares growled, but I laid a hand on his arm. "No, it's alright. Let him have me."

Ares gaped at me for a moment before he smiled, understanding that I had a plan. I walked slowly across the beach towards the stunned Apollo. He watched me in silence and then asked, "Who are you?"

I stopped walking and stared at his face. He looked like a male version of me. "I'm...Artemis," I whispered.

Apollo blinked a couple of times and then shook his head. "I've been sent here to collect you."

I scoffed. "I'm not a urine sample to be collected."

The vampire hybrids behind Apollo shifted nervously as I walked closer to their leader.

I started to reach out towards him, but a sword appeared in Apollo's hand, and I barely raised mine in time to block his strike. "Do not touch me," he growled.

"You're a halfbreed, like me," I whispered as our swords ground against each other's.

"I am nothing like you," Apollo growled as he pivoted and sliced at me.

The moment broken, the hybrids rushed towards the halfbreeds and the battle truly began. Apollo matched me strike for strike. I couldn't break through his guard, but he couldn't break through mine.

Ares appeared at my side and slashed at Apollo with his claws, but Apollo jumped backwards, and his wings popped out of his back.

Achilles ran forward and jumped into the air, his wings extending and his sword appearing in his hand.

Apollo blocked Achilles' attack, but fell to his feet on the ground.

Three hybrids rushed over to protect Apollo from us. I

decapitated one and rushed around the others who were distracted by Ares and Achilles. Apollo was ready for me though, and blocked my attack easily. I shot fire at him, but he deflected it away.

"Who are you?" I screamed at him. "Why do you look like me?"

Apollo growled, but then Darren was suddenly running down the beach towards us. I gasped, and fear made me freeze. Apollo swung his sword at me, but stopped with the edge pressed to my throat.

I whimpered, "Darren."

Apollo growled and pressed the blade harder against my throat, but still didn't draw blood. "Why don't I want to kill you? Is this some type of spell?"

Darren slowed and walked towards us. "Kill her, Apollo. Kill her now."

"You're my father! Why do you despise me so much?" I asked as tears leaked down my face. Due to my memory problem, I hadn't had time to deal with the words he had spoken to me during the battle.

"What do you mean *your* father?" Apollo asked in shock, his sword pulling slightly away from my throat.

Darren growled at Apollo who shuddered. "Kill her, Son."

"Son?" I gasped. I looked at Apollo and understood. "You're my brother."

Apollo shook his head. "No. That can't be. You told me I was your only child."

Darren groaned. "I thought maybe one of my twins could be a worthy child, but apparently, you are both worthless." Darren reached for the sword in Apollo's hand, but it disappeared into Apollo's skin. Only another Sidhe could use the swords we possessed.

"Explain this!" Apollo yelled.

Darren struck Apollo so fast that I only heard the sound and then Apollo was on the ground. I started to move towards him, but Darren grabbed me by the throat and picked me up. "If you want something done right, you have to do it yourself."

I struggled against him and then relaxed. He was my dad and it hurt that he hated me, but I was a warrior. I was a powerful being and I would not be strangled by this man. I pulled my sword up and stuck it through Darren's stomach. He looked down and laughed. "You think that little thing will kill me?" His grip tightened and black spots began covering my vision. I couldn't move. I couldn't call my power. How could this man have so much power over me?

"Ares," I gasped with what air I had left.

I heard a responding snarl and then Darren was fighting with one hand while he choked me with the other. The power he possessed was like nothing I had ever encountered before. His aura was bright red and the sheer amount of strength frightened me. Darren tossed Ares backwards and then slammed me onto the ground. He touched the sword, making it disappear from his stomach and then changed his hand to a paw. He raised his three inch claws over my throat. "Time to finish your pathetic life," he said with a snarl.

I closed my eyes and waited for death. I didn't want to die, but Darren was *too* strong. He had to be close in age to Ares. His blood called to mine and I could not kill him. I opened my eyes a moment later to see his claws stopped an inch from my throat. I held my breath to keep them from getting closer to my skin and looked from Darren's shocked face to the blade protruding from his chest, where his heart was. Darren's body fell lifelessly to the ground.

I expected to find Achilles standing behind Darren, but it

was Apollo. "None shall harm my sister," he growled.

"You saved me." I said through my hoarse throat. "Why?"

Apollo rubbed his temples and looked from me to Darren's body and back. "I…I don't know. I couldn't stand by and let him kill you. I just…my body moved on its own."

Ares growled from behind him and then Apollo took to the skies. "Fall back!" he yelled to what was left of the hybrids.

Ares started to go after him, but I grabbed his hand. "No! Let him go."

The hybrids and Apollo fled down the beach, disappearing around the turn.

Achilles squatted down next to Darren and checked his pulse. "He's dead."

I frowned down at the body. "Apollo killed him."

Achilles' eyebrows raised. "He killed his father?"

I stood and shoved my finger in his chest, pushing him backwards. "You knew? You knew he was my brother!"

Achilles stumbled back a couple steps and then caught my hands in his. "Yes, but he's our enemy," Achilles said softly.

I pointed to Darren's dead body. "Apollo saved me from Darren. Now, you tell me everything about him."

Theseus trotted up to me in his wolf form and whined. I turned away from Achilles and scratched under his chin. "What is it?"

He rubbed his head against my hand and then trotted away. I sighed and followed him to find a young halfbreed bleeding from gashes with Koda by his side putting pressure on the wounds.

I pushed him away. "Stay still." I put pressure on the wound and he winced. "It'll be over soon."

The boy nodded and then slowed his breathing as I closed my eyes. "By the blood in my veins, the power of the night, I call to the plants and ask for your help." Little bits of glowing energy danced across the wind towards me and with some focus, I pushed them into the wound. Instantly the bleeding stopped, the internal issues sealed and healed and the skin was blemish free.

"How many other spells did you learn?" demanded Victor in a near shout.

I patted the smiling boy on the head and stood up to face Victor. "Enough for me to be sure that if we can get your father and his whole army on the battlefield, I can obliterate every single vampire there."

Victor's eyes widened before he turned silently away to walk back to the house.

Theseus rubbed his head against my shoulder and I turned to smile at him. "Yes, I'm alright. No one hurt me."

Ares growled and Theseus whined in apology before backing away. I put my hands on my hips and glared at Ares. "He wasn't being possessive or overstepping bounds. He was acting as any other wolf in a pack would."

Ares' shirt was gone and as he walked towards me, the hormones I'd worked so hard to keep in control the past one hundred years surged forward. He inhaled, and I knew he could smell my desire.

Achilles turned away from us and walked into the house.

My emotions warred with me as my desire to mate with Ares and my desire to heal the feelings I'd hurt with Achilles gnawed at me.

Ares stopped an inch away from me and nipped my chin. "He understands."

My body wasn't responding to any of the commands I gave it, my arms felt like jelly, so I just nodded and allowed him to pick me up and dash off to the woods. Ares didn't stop running until we came to a densely wooded area where a bed of leaves awaited us.

I looked at it suspiciously. "Had this planned, did you?"

Ares smiled smugly. "It was only a matter of time before the need overcame your virtues. Besides, I am your mate."

He laid me down on the bed of leaves and kissed me fiercely. Everything felt so different than the first time we'd kissed and yet the same. I ran my hands along his sculpted chest and abs and to his muscular back, now slick with sweat from the fight. He nipped my shoulder, making me moan, which made him growl.

I didn't want to rush our mating, but I couldn't wait to become one with him again. I pushed him down onto his back and he laughed softly. Though I saw his eyes glint with gold, he let me force him to submit. I stood back and admired him in all his glory. "It's definitely been too long since I've seen you. I'd forgotten how magnificent you are."

Ares pulled me down and flipped us over, cushioning my head with his arms. "You almost died again today," he whispered softly as he kissed his way from my lips to my chin to my throat.

"No, I wasn't bleeding to death like all the times before."

Ares growled and nipped my chest. "If Apollo hadn't stopped him, Darren would have skewered you."

I arched up as he kissed his way down the center of my chest. "I'm sorry," I whispered.

"Say that again," he said with a hint of a growl in his voice.

I met his eyes and felt tears sliding down my face at the same time I saw tears falling down his to land on my chest. "I'm sorry, Ares."

He kissed me again and then made love to me until the sun rose above the trees.

FOURTEEN

Artemis was much different than the first time I'd met her. She was still naïve in many respects, but I could see that whatever she'd been doing the past one hundred years had definitely changed her.

The most shocking change was her incredible power. I wouldn't admit it to Ares, but if she and I battled it would be a very intense and catastrophic battle. I would win, but I would be terribly injured and drained afterwards.

I couldn't outwardly choose sides, but I hoped Artemis continued to only mate with Ares. They belonged together and no matter what Achilles said, the two of them were not soul mates like Ares and Artemis were.

"Victor?" Koda asked softly, "Are you feeling alright?"

I shook my head and stood up from the couch where I sat. "I need to feed. I'll return shortly."

Koda watched me, not convinced that I was telling the truth and thinking those thoughts loud enough that I would hear even if my focus was elsewhere. I wasn't telling the truth, but I wasn't going to tell him that. We had known each other so long that he could tell when I was lying. I was not looking forward to the days when Artemis could read me as well.

I closed my eyes and focused on my favorite place to feed. The Red Bordello, a house of humans offering themselves for vampires to feed upon. Using my power, I shifted my body from one place to the other.

A woman screamed, and I opened my eyes, smiling. "Hello, *ma chéri.*"

"Sir, you startled me," the doe-eyed petite woman said as she released her hold on her bed sheet. She had golden wheat colored hair and eyes the color of dark emeralds. Her negligee was white and she looked so fragile in the large, four poster bed.

The room was bare except for the large bed with extremely fluffy sheets and pillows. This room was where she slept so it was not as ornately decorated as the bedrooms where they entertained vampires when feeding them. I was the only one that I knew of who visited any of the feeders in their personal rooms.

I stood beside the bed, looking down on her. She had aged since the last time I was here and looked to have a bruise under her right eye. I picked her hand up and kissed it softly. "I apologize for startling you."

She smiled sweetly at me and then scooted over, patting the bed. "Sit with me a moment."

I obliged her and then turned her face to mine. "Who has harmed your lovely face?"

Most women would have turned away or been ashamed, but not her. She simply smiled and said, "It comes with the territory of being a blood whore."

I cringed, hating that term for the humans who offered

their blood for vampires. "You are too sweet to be using such vile terms."

"You are too kind for being the Prince of Vampires."

I smoothed her hair back from her neck and she shuddered in anticipation. "I wish I could stay longer, but I have much on my agenda," I whispered in her ear as I kissed it softly and then made small tender kisses along her jaw line and to her neck.

Her jugular vein pulsed faster as I kissed beside it and my fangs lengthened in response. If I was not helping Ares, I would take this girl and keep her to myself, but I could not do that now. I would not promise her or even suggest the notion until I could do it. I was not one to go back on my word and I did not want to offer until I was sure I could keep it.

She ran her hand down my arm and then arched up into me as I kissed her stomach. I pulled the bed sheets down and then found my favorite vein on the inside of her leg.

My fangs extended fully and I bit down, sucking as her blood flowed from the bite. She hissed a moment and then relaxed on her back, enjoying the emotions I was giving her. Every vampire over the age of thirty could manipulate a human's emotions to make their bite enjoyable. Some used it negatively while others just didn't use the ability. I preferred to use it, enjoying the smiles on the women's faces as I fed.

I finished my feeding and pressed against the bite to ensure it stopped bleeding. "Lie with me until I fall asleep," she ordered quietly, still high on the feeding.

I should have said no, but I wasn't going to be needed until tomorrow, if at all by Ares. She was soft and warm as I laid down beside her, and she sighed softly. I stroked her hair and whispered to her in French, knowing she couldn't understand, but enjoyed it nonetheless.

She snuggled against me and giggled quietly. "I always dreamed of sleeping with a prince."

"Then go to sleep little Princess. And dream of happier days."

I watched her sleep with a smile on her face and then teleported back to the house.

"How is she?" Koda asked from the reclining chair.

I tried to hide my smile, but he saw it and smiled back. "Someday, my friend, we will both find females."

Koda shook his head. "We both know that we've already found them. Sadly, we are both unable to have them."

I patted his shoulder and whispered, "There are many more to choose from."

He scrunched his face and whispered, "How can I look past perfection to see them?"

Achilles and I were the only ones who knew of Koda's feelings towards Artemis. And I was probably the only one who knew the true depth of his feelings for her. "You must. Or you shall only wallow in what could have been. There could be a perfect one *for you* if you would just open your eyes."

He shook his head and stood. "I think I'll go for another run."

"Do not lose yourself in the wolf's mind for too long."

He bared his teeth at me. "I know."

I watched him go, trying my hardest to block out his pain and the thoughts in his head. If he got any worse I was going to have to talk to Ares about him.

He was dangerously close to losing himself to the wolf and it would break Ares to have to kill another of his brothers. I could do it to spare him the pain, but I had to hope he would keep the human side alive.

I couldn't judge him for his fascination on one being when

I was fascinated on one, and she was human. I shook my head in disgust at myself and walked down to the basement area. The pack looked at me and then went back to their various activities. I walked to my room and lay down to sleep. Or at least to dream of what could have been.

FIFTEEN

ARTEMIS

We woke to the sounds of whispering. Ares growled next to me and wrapped his arms around me protectively. "She's sleeping," he whispered.

"We discussed this, Ares. I know I agreed not to mate with Artemis, but you're not allowing me time alone with her," said Achilles.

Ares growled again as Achilles moved closer. "Back away."

"Ares," Koda said in an exasperated tone. "Stop acting so damn possessive. It's Achilles we're talking about, not some random wolf."

Ares nuzzled my hair and exhaled. He stayed in that position for two more minutes before finally releasing me and standing up. "I'm sorry."

I rolled onto my back and stretched. "What's going on?" I asked as I feigned naivety, looking from Ares to Koda and then to Achilles.

"It's time for breakfast," said Ares softly, pulling me to my feet and kissing my cheek.

I kissed his lips and then moved to hug Koda, but my

stomach felt weird. I stopped moving and frowned as I tried to determine the problem. I stood perfectly still for thirty seconds as nothing seemed to answer what the weird sensation was. And then my stomach grumbled. I laughed at my ridiculousness and said, "I guess it *is* breakfast time." I hugged Koda before stepping into Achilles' arms. "Good morning."

Achilles smiled down at me. "Hello."

Ares and Koda took the lead and Achilles placed my hand in his as we headed back towards the house. Ares got dressed and tossed me clothes so I could dress as well before we all went down the stairs to the sub level of the house. The sub level wasn't what I had expected. I thought it would be wood and dirt and small and dark, but it was none of those things. Large wooden support beams held the sides and upper level from crashing down, but marbled tile and candelabras decorated the area. It was also much bigger than I thought it would be with two hallways leading to at least ten doors and three large main rooms, including a full kitchen.

The pack was sitting around the outer edge of the living room floor with empty plates in their hands, looking hungry. Victor stood in the center of the room tapping his foot impatiently, but once he caught sight of Ares and me, he just smiled.

Ares cleared his throat and the room quieted. "You all fought well yesterday and we're very proud. Now, let's eat!"

Five boys from the pack brought in platters of slightly cooked meat and set them down in a large circle in the center of the room. Ares picked up two empty plates and handed me one. I followed him as he took some meat from each of the platters and filled mine as well. Once our plates were full, Achilles and Koda took their turns, and then the rest of the room. Ares found an open spot against the wall and we all sat down with Ares beside Victor, me beside Ares, Achilles beside me and then Koda beside Achilles. I ate in silence as I listened to the pack around me discuss the small victory the battle was yesterday and what it could mean for the battle at large.

I finished my meat and leaned against Achilles who was sipping a glass of wine. He tilted it towards me. "Want some?"

I clapped a hand over my mouth to keep from throwing up. "No. I don't drink wine."

Ares and Koda roared with laughter. "Now, she doesn't drink wine," Koda said around his laugh.

Victor arched an eyebrow in question, and Ares said, "One night at Lyngvi she drank enough wine to get drunk and ended up throwing it all up in the toilet a few minutes later. I hadn't seen a young wolf drink so much in a long time."

I blushed and looked down at my hands. "I was upset because all those women were flirting with you and trying to kill me."

Achilles snorted. "Werewolves always have so much drama when they're together." The pack stilled and looked at him in question. He rolled his eyes. "Full blooded werewolves, not halfbreeds." The pack started talking and eating again. Achilles exhaled. "Your kind is so sensitive."

I rolled my eyes. "Right, because Sidhe are known for their loving, calm demeanors. Oh wait, that's right, I was supposed to be killed by them!"

Achilles sighed, but didn't pick up the argument. I relaxed against him to let him have his time with me near, but reached out my other hand to Ares so I could touch him as well.

Achilles smiled at me and kissed my cheek softly. I laid my head down on his shoulder and exhaled. This was heaven. I never wanted it to end.

Once everyone had finished eating, Ares called the pack

outside for training, despite my wish to cuddle. The sand was somewhat restrictive for movement, but after running in it for a few miles I started to get the hang of it. I really enjoyed the wind blowing my hair back and the taste of the sea water as it splashed beside me.

Koda waved me over from farther up the beach and I ran to him, skidding to a stop and spraying sand at him. Koda stood across from me with a wicked smile on his face. "I have a feeling you're a bit out of practice, darlin'."

I rolled my shoulders and stretched my legs. "Perhaps, but even out of practice, I'm more powerful than you."

Groups began sparring around us, practicing everything from hand-to-hand combat to dealing with four or more opponents at once.

Koda rolled his eyes. "Powers don't matter in close combat situations. I'll drop you to the ground and stake you before you can even make a fireball."

I laughed and rolled my shoulders. "Bring it."

Koda charged forward and was in a half-shift before I noticed his hand was now a paw. I blocked the hit, but he scratched my arm. I gasped as it burned and dropped down to kick at his legs. He jumped up and swung at me again. I rolled out of his reach and shot a fireball at him. He growled and patted out the flames on his shirt. I stood and prepared for his next attack, a smile lifting my lips. Koda's eyes flickered above my head and I dropped to the ground just as an arm whistled over me. I flipped over to find Ares standing over me, smiling wide.

I kicked him in the stomach and then rolled between his legs to face them. Ares nodded at Koda and then they both charged me. I jumped up and released my wings, but Ares grabbed my foot and yanked me back down to the earth. I folded in my wings and then punched him in the face as they retracted completely. Koda swung at me, and I formed my sword. Ares knocked the sword from my hand and then Koda punched me in the face. I stumbled backwards and growled at them.

I felt my skin grow hot as I began to glow and my powers released. "Enough play," I whispered. I charged forward and swept Koda's legs out from under him and then punched him in the chest as he fell to the ground. Ares swung at me, but I caught his fist in my hand and punched at him. I, however, had forgotten that no matter how much more powerful I had become, Ares was *much* more powerful than me. He grabbed my hand, flipped me on my back and pinned me to the ground. I screamed in rage at being pinned and let my wings extend from my back to toss us up and him off of me. Unfortunately, Ares was prepared for this maneuver and held on to me.

He grabbed a handful of my hair, tilted my head back and placed his teeth, which were now four elongated wolf's fangs into my throat. "Submit," he said around my throat. I whined and relaxed in his grip. Ares removed his fangs and kissed my throat. "Thank you."

I stepped out of Ares' arms and rubbed my throat while glaring at him. Koda stood up from the ground. "Dammit."

A smile twigged my lip. "At least I beat you."

Koda sighed. "Yeah, whatever."

Theseus laughed. "Dad got beat by a girl."

Koda growled, but the rest of the pack laughed with Theseus, making Koda turn bright red.

~

WE CONTINUED the same daily routine of eating, training, and sleeping for four weeks until Ares and Achilles decided to relocate. I was surprised they'd waited so long to move since Apollo knew where we were, but they didn't seem worried.

We stood outside on the beach preparing to leave so I decided then was a good time to show them the trick the dragons had taught me. "Well, are we all ready to go?"

Everyone nodded and I said, "Will everyone please crowd around us and be sure to touch each other?"

Ares looked at me quizzically, but everyone obeyed my order, even Victor and Achilles. I closed my eyes, summoned my power and said, "Try not to puke."

The dizzying vortex sucked us in and then spit us out just in front of the entrance to the Light Court. All of the members of the pack groaned as they resisted the urge to throw up. Victor, Ares and Achilles stared at me with wide eyes. Achilles asked, "Who taught you that?"

I smiled. "The dragons taught me it so I wouldn't kill Draco-Blu or Theseus in my worry over Ares before I had regained my memories. They told me it would take practice to be able to do this, but once I felt the amount of power I'd had returned to me, I knew I could do it now."

Victor whistled. "You are quite an interesting woman. Ares is going to have to keep a tight watch on you."

I rolled my eyes. "Like that's not already happening."

All of the men laughed, and Achilles opened the staircase, which I knew was actually a portal to the dimension that contained the Sidhe courts. "Single file," he said as he started down the stairs. I summoned my powers so I would glow and be able to see as I walked down the stairs and smiled when I noticed the rest of the pack doing the same.

It didn't take long for us to make it through the door and

into the open grassy field where I'd talked with Achilles the last time I'd come here. Hera was waiting for us, but as soon as Achilles walked to her, she took his arm and led him away. Erebos and Heracles stood guard and smiled at me as I stepped out. I bowed to them and they bowed back.

"Greetings, Artemis," said Erebos in his deep booming voice.

"It pleases us to see you well," said Heracles.

I smiled back. "Thank you. I am glad to see that neither of you was hurt after I was abducted."

Erebos and Heracles kept their smiles in place but did not respond. Hera and Achilles came back a moment later and Hera addressed Ares and me, "I have rooms for your pack, if you'd like my guards to show them there?"

Ares bowed his head respectfully. "I would greatly appreciate that, Queen of the Light Court."

Hera snapped her fingers and Erebos and Heracles waved the pack forward. Ares pulled me against him and held me still. "Wait, I want to show you something," he whispered.

I relaxed against his warm body and waited as the rest of the pack, including Koda and Theseus were led to the castle. Achilles glanced at us, but then turned and followed his mother.

I'm still supposed to get alone time with you too, Artemis. Don't forget. Achilles said through my mind.

I smiled. *I have not forgotten and will be sure to pencil you in.*

Ares kissed the top of my head and then began leading me through the town. Sidhe peeked out their windows at us, but if we looked, they quickly turned away. I didn't understand their aversion to us. It wasn't like we were lepers or anything crazy. We were just two mixed bloods. Sadly, I knew that being a mixed blood was exactly why they hid.

Once this was over, I intended to fix the Sidhe's belief system.

Ares wove his way expertly through the town's streets and seemed to know where he was going. I, on the other hand, was completely lost. I remembered coming here with him before, but we hadn't explored this area then.

Did it pain him to be back here? I tried to sense his feelings, but he had blocked me from them.

We made what felt like a circle around a large building and stopped. Amazingly there was a river there surrounding a small island covered in green grass, weeping willows whose branches dropped into the river and cherry trees whose pink blossoms drifted to the ground lazily. It was the most beautiful thing I'd ever seen, something straight out of a poem and yet here it was in front of me. We definitely had not visited this spot last time.

"It's beautiful," I whispered as we started across the wooden bridge to the island.

Ares stayed silent, but I could see the small smile tugging up the corners of his lips. We stepped onto the island and an immense amount of power in the plants and ground of the island pressed against me. A small sound escaped my lips as the power filled me and opened me up, my skin glowing softly and my vines sparkling.

We walked around the small island until we were underneath the cherry tree which had the most blossoms and the most power. Ares reached up and plucked one of the small pink blossoms and held it out to me. "This is an area of power. The Sidhe call the island the '*cor*' which means heart. This tree is the real center of all the power and is called '*mater*' which means mother."

I took the blossom from him and gasped as the power

drained from the blossom and into me. I staggered backwards and ended up leaning against the tree. Power poured into me like a wave of fire, scalding me from the inside. I screamed, but couldn't move away from the tree to stop the overload of power. Ares grabbed my hand, but instead of pulling me away from the tree and releasing me from the power, the power spread to him and pulled him against me and the tree.

We screamed in our shared pain and pleasure as the power scalded us and yet filled us with euphoria. I felt as though my eyes were going to pop out of their sockets from the pressure of so much power in me. The power flared and then disappeared as Ares and I fell away from the tree.

I landed on top of Ares and we both gasped for breath and moaned in pain. I started to push off of him when I realized that I wasn't the only one glowing. "Ares," I whispered.

He looked up at me and frowned. "What? What is it?"

I pointed at his body. "You…you're glowing."

I moved off of him and he quickly walked to the river, staring in shock at his reflection. I stayed sitting on the ground as my body absorbed the power the tree had given me. How was it possible that I could hold so much power in me? When I borrowed power from plants I always had to use it or it tried to destroy me, but *mater* had given me power to store. Was *mater* a cognizant being? Could she really understand and did she know battle was looming?

A noise made me look at the bridge where I could see a crowd had gathered. No doubt they'd felt the power the tree was giving us and come to see who the lucky Sidhe was. Judging by their faces, they weren't pleased.

Ares laughed suddenly, making me jump. He ran to me and picked me up, swinging me around as he hugged me.

"Ares? Why are you laughing?" I asked nervously.

He set me down and I stared at the new marks on his body. I ripped his shirt off and gasped. Ares' arms and chest were now decorated with tattoo-like, black images of running wolves. I touched one of the little black wolves and jumped as it moved, biting the wolf in front of it, and causing all of the wolves on Ares to begin to run. The wolves ran together and even yipped.

I looked up and Ares' eyes were white pearls. I'd only seen this once before when I had released Achilles' power. "How is this possible?" I asked softly.

Ares smiled. "Do you mean the fact that you are my destined mate and can activate my powers?"

I shook my head at him. "No, we both already know I'm your mate. I mean, how is it possible that you have Sidhe powers?"

"Perhaps I had them all along, but since my wolf nature was so strong it lay dormant until you activated them."

"I didn't activate them, *mater* did."

Ares cupped my face in his hands. "You are always underestimating yourself. I touched this tree thousands of times when I was young in hopes that it would do this exact thing. The only reason this happened was because you were the one I touched."

"Out of the way! Make room," Hera yelled. Ares and I turned to find Hera pushing through the crowd which had gathered. She stopped at the edge of the bridge, just a foot away from the island and gasped. "No. It cannot be."

Ares walked towards her with his arms spread. "You see it. There are others here who witnessed it. My powers have surfaced. It seems you were wrong about me."

Hera pointed at me. "You! You did this!"

I shrugged. "That's what Ares said, but I didn't do it on purpose. I would do it again though."

Hera was glaring at me and looked ready to attack, but she held her ground and kept from releasing her powers. Was she holding back because of our truce or was she frightened of how much *more* powerful I'd become?

Ares exhaled and his eyes returned to normal and his body stopped glowing. "It seems I may be able to join the Sidhe's ranks after all."

Hera glared at him. "If that is the case, then I demand that you bow to me, your queen."

Achilles was standing beside Hera and up until that point, his face had remained perfectly blank. As soon as she said it, he rolled his eyes and shook his head in disbelief.

Ares bowed his head at the neck. "I acknowledge that you are queen of this domain, but I will join my father in his Court."

Hera glared harder at Ares, her skin starting to glow softly as she grew angrier. "Very well. Come now, let's return to the Prince's quarters and discuss this upcoming battle." Hera spun on her heel and marched back through the crowd of people.

Achilles walked down the bridge to stand in front of Ares. "You look better now," Achilles teased.

Ares laughed. "Don't worry, brother, I will not try to steal your throne. I have no intention of taking your title."

Achilles frowned. "You are a Prince of the Sidhe as much as I am and you will be given that title as soon as father sees you. I was simply meaning that I much prefer your decorated Sidhe body to the boring werewolf one."

Ares was frowning, too. "You will of course be next in line for the throne though."

Achilles smiled. "Of course."

Ares held out his hand with a smile. Achilles stared at Ares' hand a moment before clasping it and then pulling Ares into a hug. Tears pricked my eyes as I watched the two men I loved hug and completely forgive each other for the first time in over four hundred years.

I realized one thing though as I stared at them. "Ares?" Ares and Achilles broke from their hug and turned to me. I waved them over, not wanting everyone to hear what I was about to say. They walked to me and the urge to touch them overtook what I needed to say. I reached out and clasped each of their nearest hands. I exhaled happily and then whispered, "Ares, I don't think you have wings."

Achilles' eyes spread wide. "She's right. Whenever she released my powers before, my wings automatically popped out." He pointed to my wings, which were out. "Even hers are out."

Ares shrugged. "It's alright. I don't like flying much anyways. I prefer the ground under my paws."

Achilles walked across the bridge and stopped when he noticed all of the angry looking Sidhe gathered. "From this day forward all shall recognize Ares, Prince of the Werewolves as Ares, Prince of the Werewolves *and* Sidhe. If any disagrees, let them challenge me."

The Sidhe gasped and then began whispering loudly to each other. Ares picked up his ripped shirt and smiled at me. "I wish this had been done in other circumstances."

I blushed and took the shirt. "I'm sorry."

He laughed and wrapped his arm around my waist. "Don't be. I liked it. Besides, I've ruined more clothes in fits of anger than you've probably ever owned in your life."

I giggled as I imagined Ares ripping his shirt off like when a comic book character gets angry and turns into a large green monster.

"What are you laughing about?" he asked.

The giggle turned into a laugh and I spoke in the deepest voice I could muster, "You won't like me when I'm angry."

Ares smiled and then lunged for me. "You think that's funny?"

"Uh oh, you better watch out! I think he's turning green!" I yelled as I jumped away from him and ran across the bridge.

Achilles laughed. "The Hulk is a rather fitting character comparison for you, Ares."

Ares snorted, a sound much better suited to his canine form. "I don't turn green."

"No, but you do get furry and rip your shirts off," I answered as another fit of laughter took me and I had to stop to hold my stomach.

"I think I'm more like Wolverine," Ares said seriously.

"Well you are grumpy like him and way too full of your-self," Achilles said in the same serious tone as Ares.

Ares flexed his abdominals and then lifted his arms, flexing his biceps and chest. "Have you seen me? How can I not be full of myself?"

My laughter disappeared as I looked at him. He was defi-nitely way too perfect.

"Now you look like Koda," Achilles said with a chuckle.

Ares swung at Achilles, but he jumped back and Ares growled.

"Run, he's turning green!" Achilles said and grabbed my hand, running down the bridge with me in tow. A new fit of laughter forced me to stop running as I was bent over holding my stomach with tears falling down my face.

"Ha. Ha. Very funny," Ares said as he caught up to us.

Hera appeared in front of me. "Why are you delaying? Come, let's get on with our planning. We don't have much time."

I stopped laughing and took a couple of deep breaths to calm down before I let the anger control my tongue. "I apologize for enjoying the renewed time with my mate. I forgot that the world revolves around you, Your Highness."

Achilles groaned softly and Ares sighed. Hera's face turned red, but for once she held her tongue. She held out her hands and Ares and Achilles each took one and then took my hands. Hera started to draw power in, but I beat her to it and teleported us into her court room where she conducted her important business. We landed in front of a large conference table and eyes popped open from all of the Sidhe and half-breeds gathered.

Hera's face was the most priceless of all. "You can teleport?"

I smiled. "A gift from the dragons to me for my friendship."

Several of the Sidhe gasped. Hera's face paled and she asked, "You're friends with dragons?"

I pulled out Blu's scale and showed it to the room. "I am."

"Perhaps now is not the time for this discussion? Let's work on our plan for the battle," said Achilles in a strong and demanding voice.

Victor sat in one of the many chairs and nodded. "Yes, we need to discuss strategy."

I dropped into one of the chairs. "Do we really need a strategy? We just need to have Maurice and as many of his vampires in the area so I can toast them. Wham, Bam, Thank you Ma'am and we've won."

"You think you're so powerful?" asked a female Sidhe with green filigree designs around her eyes. She obviously didn't like me and her glare was most impressive despite her small frame and delicate, doll-like face.

I covered my hand in sunlight and smiled as I said, "I know I am."

Victor nodded. "Yes, she is, but the problem is getting my father to the battleground. He prefers to let others fight his battles."

I shrugged, releasing the sunlight. "Then we storm his home and I toast him."

Koda sighed. "Darlin' it won't be easy like last time. Last time he was trying to capture you to make you his. Now, he just wants you dead."

"So how do we get him on the battlefield then?" I frowned.

"We have to offer him something he can't refuse," said Ares quietly.

Victor gasped. "No. There are too many variables and too many things that could go wrong."

"You think I don't know that?!" yelled Ares. "Unless you can come up with a better plan, that's the only way."

"We need to fight a battle which we lose first and then do that," said Victor.

"No! We cannot lose a battle on purpose. That would mean letting our people die!" I yelled.

"Artemis," Achilles started.

I stood up from my chair and slapped my hands down on the table. "No! I will not sacrifice anyone. We can fight one battle and then discuss whatever it is that Ares wants to do. We do not have to lose that first battle though. I can refrain from using my sunlight magic and that way Maurice won't know I can do it."

The room was silent for several minutes until Hera said, "I agree with Artemis. We can fight this first battle no matter the outcome. I would like to know what it is that Ares is suggesting."

Ares looked at the table a moment and then said, "The only way I can foresee Maurice coming out to the battlefield is if we agree to surrender and to give Artemis to him as a good faith gift."

"You want to give him Artemis?" Hera asked softly.

Ares smiled. "Well we wouldn't *really* be giving her to him, but we could make it look authentic. I could be bound and guarded by several of your Sidhe warriors while Artemis is bound with her hands in front of her. Then when Maurice takes the bait and comes near her, she can fry him and those nearest him."

"I like it," I said with a smile on my face.

Koda laughed. "You would like that idea."

"What's that supposed to mean?" I asked with a glare in his direction.

He held his hands up in surrender. "Nothing. Never mind."

Ares pulled me down into my seat and kissed the back of my hand. "Calm down. You're getting excited over nothing."

I took a deep cleansing breath. "Sorry."

"When will your pack be ready for the first battle?" Hera asked.

I looked at Ares' smiling as he said, "We're ready now, but you should begin the preparations of your Sidhe. We need to get word out that we're looking for a fight."

Victor smiled. "I'll spread word of that. I still have some allies who are undercover with my father's side."

Hera nodded. "Good. I'm sure the vampires will act quickly once they know we have Artemis with us again. I'll have Hephaistos start on the weapons."

SIXTEEN

The full moon hung above us. Her presence made me itch to run as a wolf with my pack and hunt beneath her soothing and powerful light. I decided then that I would get the pack together and go for a run that night. I didn't feel right not having run with the halfbreed pack yet. A soft breeze blew around me, swirling cherry blossoms in a soft, soothing whirlwind. Energy from the blossoms seeped into me and filled me with a low level of power. My skin tingled and glowed softly as I absorbed the power and stuffed it down into the imaginary box that I pictured hiding within my soul. Over the last week, I'd been storing power there slowly, every time I visited the island.

"Artemis?" Achilles called from somewhere within the houses.

"Yes?" I answered, not bothering to move from my spot or raise my voice.

He walked around the house nearest the bridge that crossed to the island. He slowly made his way across the bridge and stopped in front of me. "Ares shouldn't have showed you this island. You're spending more time here than with us lately."

I held open my arms and he sat down, leaning against me and letting me hold him. It wasn't a common gesture from me to him and he didn't delay in accepting it. "I'm sorry. I know I need to spend more time with you, but I've just needed some time to meditate and think."

He turned and pulled me into his arms, reversing our position and leaning me against his chest. "It's alright, Sweetheart. I've just been worried about you because you've been blocking me from your thoughts so deliberately." He slowly stroked my hair, calming me even more than my meditation had. Gently he titled my chin up and kissed me.

My control slipped the more time I spent touching him. Each additional time I touched him, the more I wanted to give in to him. His hands slid up and down my arms as he kissed me and I could feel the strength in them. My head swam, rendering logical thoughts impossible and allowing my hormones to rage. I turned completely around, wrapping my legs around his sides and sitting on his lap. I fisted my hands in his hair, loving the silky smoothness against my skin and kissed him deeply. He moaned and the sound made me smile and growl happily. He picked me up and then laid me down on the ground. The feel of him lying on top of me was incredible. I had wanted it for so long, but had been denying us both.

Was he as talented as Ares? The thought stopped me cold and dispersed my hormones. I couldn't cheat on Ares. If I mated with Achilles it would crush Ares. I put my hand on his chest and whispered, "Wait."

Achilles sighed, stood up and turned away from me. "I wondered how long until you pushed me away."

The raw pain in his voice hurt me. "Achilles, I'm sorry. I just…"

"Stop, just stop. Please, just leave."

His voice was so full of anger and pain that I actually flinched and took an involuntary step back. I headed towards the bridge, but stopped at the beginning of it. "I'm sorry I can't love you like you deserve, but know that I do love you. If I could release you from our binding so you could find a woman who loved you, I would."

He didn't move or acknowledge me, so I left him alone. The calm I'd gained was replaced by a depression and despair that soured my mood. If my life had been a cartoon, a storm cloud would be hovering over my head raining on me. I ignored the Sidhe watching me walk through the town towards the training grounds. Let them look. Let them talk. I didn't care.

Koda and Ares smiled at me from where they were fighting as I walked onto the grassy training ground. For the first time I ignored them, not returning their smiles and walked to a deserted corner of the field as far away from everyone else as I could. I needed to release this anger and despair. I needed release from the pain.

I inhaled, pulling my fire from my core and covered my hands in it. Ares walked closer to me, but I ignored him and his presence. I tilted my head up to look at the sky and raised my hands up over my head.

I had been making headway with Achilles. I'd been able to make him smile daily, even without mating with him. And with one word, one touch, I'd erased all of that.

I always screwed things up. I hurt Ares. I hurt Achilles. I even hurt Koda. All I wanted was to please them and I failed miserably at it. The anger and gnawing ache I felt grew unbearable. Tears streamed down my face and pain gripped my body. I closed my eyes and pictured each of their faces and the times that I'd hurt them. I took another deep breath and then screamed as I shot fire up into the air. The force of the power I was using, the pain I was feeling and the sadness sent me to my knees. I sobbed uncontrollably as I released it all and screamed and cried.

I reined in the power and dropped my hands to the ground, continuing to sob. Warm arms wrapped around me and pulled me against an even warmer body. "It's alright, Darlin'. It's going to be alright," whispered Koda.

I buried my face into his chest and snuggled into him as I continued to cry. "I'm always failing. I fail at being a woman. I fail at being a mate. I fail at being a pack mate. I fail at all of the relationships around me. How can anyone think that I won't fail at this prophecy that supposedly surrounds me?"

Ares squatted down in front of me. "What happened, Artemis? What made you feel this way?"

I turned away from him and whispered, "I've hurt you all. I've hurt all three of you. All I want to do is love you and make you happy and I can't even do that."

"You do make us happy. The sight of your face makes us happier than we have been in a hundred years," whispered Koda.

I shook my head. "I'm continually causing you pain by a wrong word or a wrong decision. I can't seem to do anything right."

"Life is all about learning from your mistakes. You think I'm perfect? You sure as hell know Ares isn't perfect," Koda said as he rubbed my back slowly.

"Hey," Ares protested. He reached forward and touched my arm. "We all make mistakes. The defining factor is how you handle the mistakes and what you do to try not to make them again."

"How can I not make a mistake when the choice will hurt one person no matter what?" I whispered.

"This is about Achilles, isn't it?" Ares asked. I didn't respond which was answer enough for him. "I know it's hard and I wish there was a way I could fix it for you, but I can't. I'd be lying if I told you it wouldn't bother me if you mated with him and I won't lie to you."

"What's going on?" Achilles asked with pain still evident in his voice. *Why hadn't I felt him approach or even heard him approach? It was odd that I hadn't been able to at least feel him when he was so close.*

I stood up and brushed myself off. "Nothing." I walked away from them all and towards Erebos who was sparing with Theseus. "Greetings, Erebos," I said as I smiled at him.

He smiled at me. "Greetings, Artemis. How may I help you this day?"

"Could you teach me some advanced magic techniques?" I asked.

Erebos blinked twice and then said, "I'm not sure that I can teach you anything. You know quite a bit more than me, actually."

"I know witch magic and the magic I picked up, but I don't know much Sidhe magic," I answered.

He rubbed his chin a moment and then said, "Well, I could teach you a few of my special talents and some of the nature magic. It might be better if we had a few Sidhe who each possessed different abilities."

"Whatever you think is best."

He smiled. "I'll round up some Sidhe and meet you back here after lunch. Is that okay?"

"Thank you." I said with a smile.

Theseus touched my arm gently as I went to turn around. "Are you alright?" he asked softly.

I patted his hand reassuringly. "I'll be fine. Eventually."

He wanted to say something else, I could tell, but I walked away before he could. I could feel Ares, Achilles and Koda watching me, but I ignored them. I needed to be away from them for a while. I walked to a halfbreed and a full werewolf sparring with each other. "Mind if I join?" I asked them.

They turned and bowed to me. "Princess," they said at the same time.

I waved my hand dismissively at them. "Call me Artemis. We're pack members so there's no reason we can't be on a first name basis."

The male werewolf on the left was quite possibly the tallest man I'd ever met. His body was corded with muscle and if I hadn't heard him speak just now, I would have thought he could only scream at people. He did have bright green eyes that showed intelligence though and he looked older than the most of the others. "I'm Thor."

I swallowed my laugh and asked, "And how old are you, Thor?"

He frowned a moment in concentration and then turned to Ares who was standing across the field watching us. "How long ago did we meet?"

Ares looked down at the ground as he thought. "We met around eight hundred Anno Domini I believe."

Thor nodded, turning back to me. "So then I am around seventeen hundred years old." He frowned a moment and then nodded again. "Yes, that sounds about right."

I turned and looked at Ares, wanting to ask how old he was

since he was older than Thor, but then remembered I was trying to ignore them. I turned back to Thor. "Well, then I shouldn't be a problem against you." I looked up his massive frame. "Not that I thought I could beat you physically anyways."

The halfbreed was a woman who looked no older than twenty, but the looks she gave me made me think she was much wiser than me. "What's your name?" I asked.

She smiled. "I'm Daisy Mae," she said with a thick Southern accent. "It's a pleasure meeting you."

I shook her extended hand and smiled sweetly at her. "I love your accent. It's a pleasure meeting you, too."

"Why aren't you just the sweetest thing ever? How old are you?" she asked.

"I'm over one hundred years old," I replied. "And how old are you?"

"Only twenty-nine," she said with the sweetest smile on her face. "I'm one of Koda's daughters."

I stepped forward and hugged her. "Well, then this is a more appropriate way to greet you."

She laughed and squeezed me tight before letting me step back. "I've heard so much about you. I am so happy I finally got to meet and talk with you."

I didn't want to be rude, but I wasn't exactly in the mood to socialize. "It's a pleasure to meet you, Daisy Mae." I turned to Thor. "So, how about that fight?"

Thor sized me up, looking from the top of my head to my toes. "You sure?"

I smiled, but it came out more as a baring of teeth. "Yes."

He smiled at me, apparently pleased at my reaction. "What are the ground rules?"

"No half-shifts, I don't need you bigger than you already

are. Magic is permitted, but no lethal kinds. This is just a match for fun and to hone my skills."

Thor smiled wide, his teeth lengthening as he did. "Sounds fun. How about we start in full shift?"

I stripped my shirt off over my head and tossed it to Daisy Mae. "Sounds good." I pulled my bra, pants and panties off and gave them to Daisy Mae, too, and then dropped to my hands and knees as I shifted. The shift was smooth and pain free, but moving into my wolf form brought forth the feelings I'd suppressed. I clenched my teeth together as I fought the rage that tried to surface.

Thor yipped at me, and I turned to face him. He was almost as big as Ares, but still slightly shorter. A fight between the two of them could be catastrophic. I wagged my tail to show him I was fine and then crouched down and began circling him.

He circled with me with slow, graceful movements. I had no idea how an animal as big as he could be graceful, while I was such a klutz. He sprang at me, and I rolled to the right, spinning around and snapping at his flank, but he dodged before I could get him.

He was good. Fast and agile. I was incredibly outmatched. If this had been a real battle a smart wolf would roll on her back and beg for mercy. This wasn't a real battle though and I wasn't particularly smart. I charged forward, straight for his face and then slid underneath him, snapping my jaws around his forepaw. He yipped in pain and then spun around to attack me. I backed out from under his body, releasing his leg and danced around him.

You're good, but you're too slow. He said to me.

I lifted my lips in a snarl and smile. *Then why haven't you caught me yet?*

He lunged forward, his teeth flashing just to the right of my neck as I darted under his front legs and out the side. I knew he wasn't trying his hardest and it was only a matter of time before he caught me, but I would make him work to catch me.

He darted forward, and I barely had time to run away. I ran around him and bit his tail. He growled and before I could get away, jumped on top of me, pinning me to the ground.

This is cheating! I yelled indignantly. *A real wolf would never fight like this!*

Ah, but we are not real wolves, are we? I struggled underneath him, trying to get away, but he held me down. *Do you give up?*

NEVER! I yelled just before I whined.

"Step off of my mate, Thor," Ares said in a menacing tone from nearby. I couldn't see him since Thor was pinning my head to the ground with his neck.

I growled at Ares to butt out, but Thor stood up off of me. *You don't have to listen to him.*

Thor shook his head. *He is beta. I have to listen to him.*

I exhaled. *Sorry.*

Thor nudged my shoulder with his nose. *Did I hurt you?*

No. Just irritated that he stepped in when you weren't hurting me.

It's his place to protect you. He heard you whine and therefore thought I might be hurting you. He knows I would never purposefully harm you, but accidents do happen. What would you like to do now?

I shifted forms and took my clothes from Daisy Mae. "I think I'll go take a bath. Thank you for sparring with me. I look forward to sparring with you further in human form soon."

Thor bowed his wolf head and trotted over to his clothes.

"Are you hurt?" Ares asked from behind me.

I finished zipping my pants up and walked away, ignoring him. I shouldn't be mad at Ares, but I just wanted some time without them hovering over me. I couldn't even play fight with a member of the pack without him intervening.

My body was surprisingly sore so instead of walking, I teleported from the training grounds into Achilles' room. The room was thankfully empty and the wall where the vampires had attacked years before was blessedly fixed. I stripped my clothes off and started the water for the bathtub.

I was standing outside of the tub watching it fill up when I felt him behind me. "You know I can sense you so why bother sneaking up?"

"I'm concerned for you and I wasn't sneaking, I was just being quiet," Ares answered.

I stayed in my position, not facing him even though I needed his touch. I needed a bath and time to process my feelings as well though.

"Achilles told me what happened," he said softly.

There had been no inflection in his voice. So, either he was hiding what he was feeling, or he wanted me to ask. *Do I give in and ask, or do I stand here silently?*

I blew out air through my nose and gave in. It wasn't Ares' fault I was in a predicament. "And?"

"I understand why you're so upset now. It must have taken a lot to refuse him once you got that far. What made you do it?"

"You," I whispered as tears leaked out of my eyes silently. "I couldn't bear the thought of hurting you. Yet all I did was hurt Achilles."

Ares stepped in front of me, blocking my view of the tub with his chest. "I can't make this decision for you, Artemis. I don't know what the right answer is or what I should tell you to do. I love you and I'm a very jealous man. I don't want to share you, but at the same time I don't like seeing you or Achilles in pain."

I looked up into his face and saw the anger and pain twisting his handsome features. "You're my mate, my *passt genau*. How can I cheat on the only man that's ever given me a home?"

"He is your mate and *passt genau* as well."

I shook my head. "He's not my *passt genau*. You know it and I know it and Achilles knows it. I may be his destined mate because I released his powers, but that is different from the connection we have. I feel Achilles in my heart and my head, but I feel you in my bones and my soul. You may both share my heart, but only you have my soul."

Before I could wrap my arms around Ares, he squashed me in a hug, bruising my lips with his intense kiss. In two seconds my despair evaporated and the love Ares felt for me seeped in to lift my mood. He pulled back and wiped my eyes. "I love you, Artemis Lupine. I just wish I could fix this. I wish there were a way to make us all happy."

"If you let her mate with me that would help," Achilles said from the bathroom doorway.

"How long have you been there?" I asked in shock. *And why hadn't I felt him arrive for the second time in less than an hour?*

"Perhaps because you were too busy with Ares' tongue in your mouth," Achilles replied tautly.

I jerked at his hostility. "Achilles."

He rubbed his face and then slammed his fist into the wall. "I'm sorry, Artemis. This pain is eating me up. I can't sleep. I can't eat. All I can think about is you and the bond we have yet to complete."

"It is not fair for you to lay this burden upon her. She just returned to us!" Ares said as he pushed me slightly behind him. He was acting protective of me from Achilles, which was a very bad sign.

"She just returned to us and already you have mated with her! I know I agreed not to mate with her, but I had no idea how hard it would be," Achilles said as he stared at Ares.

Sensing I was not needed for this argument, I climbed into the now full tub and turned the water off. The warm water felt amazing against my skin and I relaxed into it. I had no idea what to say to Achilles or how to fix this issue, so I closed my eyes and relaxed, trying to ease the pain I was feeling.

"You are just being selfish and keeping her to yourself!" Achilles yelled.

"Listen to yourself! She's only back for a month and you're already pushing her and pressuring her!" Ares responded.

"You would be doing the same thing in my position!"

"I would be arguing with *you*, but not pressuring her and causing her pain! A male does not cause his female pain!" Ares bellowed, the walls shaking with the power which was leaking out as his control waned.

Achilles jerked as if the words had pained him. I clenched my eyes tighter, wishing to disappear. "Artemis? Is he right? Have I caused you pain?"

I didn't want to answer. I couldn't lie to him because he'd be able to tell. I couldn't tell him the truth without him getting upset. "Why can't we go back to how it was two days ago? Everyone was happy. Everyone was sharing well. Can't we just erase today and pretend it didn't happen?" Without a word Achilles spun around and left. This time I could feel him and his anger as he turned. "Achilles! Wait!" I called, standing up in the tub.

"Let him be, Artemis. He needs time to think," Ares said as he turned to face me. I could tell it hurt him to argue with Achilles so, but we both knew it was necessary.

"*I* needed time to think and no one left *me* alone," I complained as I settled back into the tub.

Ares smiled and grabbed the sponge and liquid soap. "I'm sorry, Sunshine, but I can't stand leaving you alone when you're in pain." He pulled a stool out from under the bathroom sink and sat down on it behind me.

"What are you doing?" I asked as he dipped the sponge in the water and squirted soap on it.

He pushed my head forward gently and then made slow, soft circles on my back. "I am washing your back."

I wanted to object and yet, I didn't. I loved it when he washed me. "I wish you hadn't intervened when I was fighting Thor," I whispered as he washed down my right arm.

"You whined and instinct overruled logic. I couldn't stand there and watch another male pin you under him while you whined."

He moved to my other arm, and I asked something I'd wanted to know since my memory had returned. "Did you ever discover the true reason for Matt's betrayal? Who it was they had?"

"Yes," Ares answered curtly and then stayed silent as he rinsed my back and arms off.

"And?" I prodded.

"And it doesn't matter anymore," he said.

"Ares."

He sighed and set the sponge down. I turned around and crossed my arms on the top of the tub and looked up into his eyes as he told me what had happened.

"The dhampirs took a female wolf he was fond of and held

her prisoner. They beat her bloody and then sent him pictures. It would have been a simple matter for me to have Victor help us extricate her, but Matt tried to solve it on his own when we were in France and they caught him. I asked Victor about the girl when I found out, but that wasn't until we were at the Dragon's Lair, and he informed me that she had been killed a week after we left France. No matter what Matt would have done for them, the girl was dead."

No wonder he had been acting so differently. I would have sacrificed almost anyone to get Ares back. "Poor Matt," I whispered.

Ares growled. "The end result was his fault. Had he come to me early on I could have saved her and his life. I do not regret punishing him for his betrayal. No one who betrays the werewolves deserves to live among us."

He was sincere and yet I heard the bitterness in his voice. He wasn't only angry at Matt and the people who caused it, but he was mad at himself as well. "Ares, it's not your fault."

Ares sighed and leaned his forehead against mine. "I wish I believed that."

"If you think about it, it was my fault. If you hadn't been distracted by me and my immaturity, then you would have noticed…"

Ares grabbed my chin and stared into my eyes. "Stop. Matt's death was not your fault."

"He was jealous of us, Ares. He wanted to be loved like you love me. He was jealous of how much time you spent with me instead of him. I could see it, but I didn't say anything to you."

"What he did was his own decision. He betrayed you and tried to hand you to Maurice. No one should do that to a pack mate, especially not a pup like you had been. Do not blame yourself for another's reckless actions," he whispered as he stared deeply into my eyes.

I smiled at him and whispered, "You should take your own advice, Alpha."

Ares smiled and kissed my lips softly. "You've become very wise since I first met you."

"Being one hundred will do that to you," I whispered as I looked down at the water.

Suddenly water splashed over the side of the tub as Ares climbed in with me, wrapping his arms around me and holding me against him. "I tried to find you. I searched all over the world and threatened hundreds of people, but no one had seen you. Achilles couldn't find you with your bond either. It was as though you were invisible. I can't imagine how hard it must have been for you all these years. If I could take them all back I would."

I nuzzled his neck and kissed it softly. "I know."

SEVENTEEN

ARTEMIS

Over the days that followed, I continued sparring with Thor, and Erebos brought Sidhe out to teach me Sidhe magic I did not yet know. I was learning quite a lot in a short amount of time and I could tell they were impressed by me. Slowly my reputation built within the Sidhe community and changed from fear and hatred to awe and respect.

After a long training session, I sat on the ground and ran my fingers through the grass to calm myself. My training group dispersed and Achilles and Ares walked to my side. "We should visit Father," Achilles said with a smile on his face.

Ares nodded. "Alright."

I smiled and grabbed each of their hands. "Ready?" They nodded and I teleported us to the front steps of the castle. The two werewolf guards jumped in surprise and then bowed when they recognized Ares and Achilles.

Achilles led the way through the castle to his father's chambers where he knocked loudly on the door.

The door opened a moment later and Zeus stood before us with his long, white beard and handsome face. His power was extremely impressive, pressing down upon me in a way I hadn't noticed the last time I'd been here, which was strange.

Achilles stood in front of Ares who stood in front of me. I wanted to move forward, but Ares gripped my hand to still me.

"Achilles! Ares! My sons! To what do I owe the honor of your visit?"

Ares stepped around Achilles, spreading his arms and said, "Looks like I'm Sidhe after all."

Zeus' eyes widened in astonishment and then he regained composure long enough to pull Ares into a hug. "I knew you had powers."

He released Ares, and I stepped around Achilles. "Hi, Zeus."

Zeus' eyes met mine and he stepped around Ares quickly. He looked at Achilles and Ares and then back at me. "Artemis? You...you found her?"

Ares smiled. "Yes, Dad, it's her."

I smiled. "Yeah, they found me and made me whole again." I spread my arms out and released my Sidhe power, letting my wings out. I flapped my wings and wiggled my fingers. "All one piece again."

He grabbed my arms and pulled me into a hug, which nearly crushed my ribs. "I thought I'd never see you again."

I pulled my wings back in and relaxed into his hug. Why did he make me feel so at peace? Was it because he was Ares' and Achilles' dad? Or because he was the king of half of my bloodline?

He pulled back and looked at my face. "Your power has greatly increased. It's amazing." I felt a push against my body, like a person leaning on me and then it was gone. "By the goddess, how did you obtain so much power?"

I stepped back from him to stand between Ares and Achilles. "I gained some while I was without my memories and more from the dragons and then I gained most of what I have from *mater* when I channeled the rest of it to Ares."

Zeus stared at me for several moments and then clapped his hands together. "This is wonderful! We need a feast!" He snapped his fingers and two beautiful Sidhe women stepped out of his chambers to stand beside him. He turned to them and said, "Prepare a feast in honor of the return of Artemis and to honor Ares now taking his rightful place as Prince."

The women bowed and scurried away to do his bidding.

"Come, you must tell me everything that has happened!" said Zeus as he put his arms around Ares' and Achilles' shoulders and pulled them away from me and into his chambers.

I followed behind them, a smile nearly splitting my face. Zeus sat down in his large, overstuffed chair and waved his sons and me over to a large couch. I sat down between Ares and Achilles and leaned against Achilles' side while Ares held my hand.

Zeus smiled at me and then said, "Artemis can you tell me where you've been the past one hundred years?"

I nodded. "For the first forty or so I was in wolf form running with wolf packs."

"Wolf packs? You mean you were with werewolves and they didn't contact Ares?" Zeus asked in shock.

I shook my head. "No, I mean wolf packs, like the actual animal."

His eyebrows raised. "Oh."

"I don't know this part of the story myself, but Selene said that they'd been hearing about an unusually large wolf in a local pack which wasn't afraid of people. Then they got reports of a naked girl seen begging for food and they were worried the vampires would get me. So, Selene decided that as a friend of the werewolves, it was her job to investigate. What she found was me separating from the wolf pack and trying to become human again. You see, I hadn't changed out of my wolf form in forty years so I couldn't even remember how to speak, and I barely remembered how to change forms. She thought I'd been abused by vampires or was on the run.

"As you can imagine, I wasn't in the best shape when she found me. My body was filthy, my hair was matted and I had lice and fleas. She recognized that I had inherited witch's powers by the woman who had cursed my father so she took me in as a witch so that she could bypass contacting the werewolves or the vampires. She crafted a pendant which could hide my smell and my skin designs and made me for all intents and purposes human."

Ares exhaled. "Well, that explains a lot."

Achilles nodded. "Yes, it does."

I continued. "I lived with her coven for sixty years and was assigned as the youth counselor to help the young members of our coven come into their powers. I only left the coven's walls to go to the magic shop when Selene needed special items. That's when Ares first spoke to me."

Ares smiled. "Yes, and then you had your dragon attack me."

I frowned. "He didn't attack you and besides, he knew who you were and I didn't. He knew who you were because you killed off most of the dragons before."

"Most of the dragons? You have a dragon?" Zeus asked as he gaped.

Achilles nodded. "We went to the Lair for their assistance in removing the block on Artemis' memories. There were at least two hundred dragons in the Lair alone."

"Draco-Blu has thirty dragons in his flight," I said softly as my heart ached at the separation of Blu.

"We could visit him if you wanted to," Ares said quietly. "Of course it would have to be after the battle."

I smiled. "Thank you, but I know we have more pressing matters."

Achilles smoothed my hair back and kissed my forehead. "We could ask them to assist us in the battle. They'd be wonderful allies and the vampires would never expect it."

"Except that Apollo knows that Draco-Blu is a friend of mine," I said softly. "He also knows I can use the sunlight magic."

"Apollo? Sunlight magic?" Zeus asked his eyes expanded to their limit.

Achilles laughed. "There's still a lot you don't know."

"Apparently," Zeus said. "What is this talk of Apollo?"

"My twin's alive. He saved me from our father as he was trying to kill me," I said softly. "I don't think Apollo's all bad. I think…" I stopped talking because I knew what Ares would say. "And while at the coven I learned to use sunlight like I do fire."

"Can you show me?" Zeus asked curiously.

I put my hands out, palms facing each other and focused on the center of them. Picturing the bright orange sun and remembering the feel of sunlight on my skin, I called the power and a small orb appeared between my hands.

Zeus walked forward and ran his hand around the orb. "Incredible. It's been centuries since I've heard of someone being able to do this."

Achilles put his hand under the orb and asked, "Can you drop it into my hand? I want to see if I can control it."

I released the ball and the orb dropped onto Achilles' hand and then dissipated.

"So much for that idea," Achilles said in a light voice, but I could see the anger in his eyes. He didn't like not being able to do magic that I could.

I leaned against Ares and felt my eyelids droop. "Why am I tired?"

Ares stroked my hair and whispered, "You've been through a lot the past few days. You should rest. I'll tell the rest of the story to Zeus." I nodded and laid my head on Ares' lap and my legs across Achilles' legs. Ares started talking and the world faded into dreams of running through the woods with Ares and Koda.

EIGHTEEN

Ares woke me up a few hours later to attend the feast that Zeus had prepared, a feast coordinated to formally proclaim Ares as Prince of the Sidhe, second in line to the throne of the Dark Court.

I stood on the dais between Ares and Achilles and fought the yawn trying to come out. A short, rotund, brown colored Sidhe woman had come and forced a Renaissance era dress on me. I liked the dress, but would have preferred jeans. Ares and Achilles had changed into soft breeches that tied in the front and button up shirts. I asked the woman why she didn't give them puffy pirate shirts and she had scowled at me and stomped off. Some people have no sense of humor.

Zeus was wearing skin tight breeches like Ares' and Achilles' and a white shirt which showed off part of his upper chest. On him, the outfit looked stunning and very fitting. Who knew the God of Lightning would look best in Renaissance clothes?

"Thank you all for gathering on such short notice today. This is a joyous day in many regards," began Zeus. He gripped

Ares' shoulder and smiled brightly. "My son, Ares, has released his Sidhe powers. He is now a member of the Sidhe realm and a prince of the Dark Court!"

The crowd clapped and a couple of the younger Sidhe cheered.

Zeus turned to me and extended his hand. I walked to him, being careful not to trip and embarrass myself. Zeus gripped my hand and said, "The second and most exciting revelation is the return of Artemis Lupine of the Sidhe and Werewolves." The crowd gasped and began murmuring. Zeus raised his hand and they stopped talking. "After being lost to us and as well as to herself, Artemis has returned and rightfully claims her title as mate of Prince Ares and Prince Achilles." The crowd clapped, but I got a few dirty looks from a couple of the Sidhe women. I rolled my eyes. I was not dealing with that again. Fighting jealous women was not fun and I'd already had more than enough of that at Lyngvi, the Werewolf home.

Zeus snapped his fingers and a beautiful bracelet appeared in his hand. It was made of thin strips of white wood braided together and it appeared to be holding a powerful spell. Zeus slipped it on to my wrist announcing, "So that you will never be lost to us again."

Achilles laughed and then pretended to cough. *He just put a tracking device on you.*

I smiled at Zeus and kissed his cheek. "Thank you."

Zeus released me, and I stood back between Ares and Achilles. Ares whispered, "Why hadn't I thought of that?"

I reached over and pinched his leg, making him rub the spot and smile.

"Let's eat!" Zeus yelled.

The tables in front of the crowd suddenly filled with food.

I knew many forms of magic and had seen many spells used, but I had never seen that before.

"How? What?" I asked in shock.

Zeus winked at me. "I've got a few tricks up my sleeve too, daughter."

Did he just call me daughter? When I got over the initial shock, I smiled. I liked the idea of being his daughter. Ares picked my hand up and led me to the head table where Zeus, Ares, Achilles and I would eat. We ate a delicious feast of every kind of animal and at least ten types of desserts. I felt like I was going to pop by the time I finished stuffing my stomach.

I exhaled, feeling content, and leaned back. "I haven't eaten like that in a long time."

Ares smiled. "The Sidhe definitely know how to throw a party."

Achilles tapped my shoulder, and I turned to find him standing and half bowing. "May I have this dance?"

"There's no music playing," I said with a frown.

Achilles clapped his hands and a troupe of musicians walked in the side doors with instruments. "You were saying?"

I shifted nervously in my seat. "I don't know how to dance."

Achilles grabbed my hand and pulled me up and out of my seat. "Then I shall teach you." Ares growled and Achilles stopped, turning to face him. "Ares, please."

Ares exhaled and looked up at the ceiling. "Two dances and then we trade off."

Achilles half bowed to him in thanks and then twirled me out onto the dance floor.

"I don't know how to dance, Achilles and I especially don't know how to do that fancy dancing that everyone here is doing," I said nervously as I looked at the other couples around us.

Achilles smiled down at me and placed one of my hands on his shoulder and held the other. "All you need is a man taught properly and dominant enough to lead. Just relax and let yourself feel the music."

He spun us around and surprisingly I didn't trip over my own feet. I smiled up at him and let him lead as we waltzed along with the other couples. The music was incredibly beautiful and with Achilles leading me, I was left to simply enjoy it all.

He smiled brightly at me and said, "See, you can dance."

I laughed. "At least that is what everyone else thinks right now."

He winked. "I won't tell if you don't."

He made me twirl, and I laughed as the colors of everything around us blurred. He stopped my twirling and pulled me against him, holding me tightly to his body with an arm around my lower back.

I stared into his eyes and saw such passion and love in them that it made my breath catch. We stood still in the center of the twirling and waltzing around us and yet none of the noise and movement mattered to me in that moment. He bent down and kissed my lips softly, sending a pleasant electric surge through my body. I kissed him back and then leaned away. "How do we dance to this song?" I asked, in an effort to change the subject from our kiss.

Achilles smiled and led me in a strange dance. We kicked our legs, spun away from each other, he dipped me and then we looped arms and all of the couples switched from partner to partner until we returned to our original dance partner. I laughed as we performed the moves and the music made me forget all of my troubles. The song ended, and I curtsied to Achilles as the other women did the same to their partners.

Achilles kissed the back of my hand and smiled at me from his bowing position. "Thank you for the dances." He took my hand and gave it to Ares who was next to us.

Ares smiled at me. "You looked gorgeous out there."

"That was all Achilles. I don't even know how to perform these dances," I said as a new song started and Ares placed our hands in the appropriate positions.

"Then I shall make you look even better," he said with a smile.

He walked us into a circle of other couples, and we all joined hands. This dance was much more synchronized than the others. "What is this dance?" I asked as I learned the repetitive moves. *Step side to side, release hands and dance in a small circle, kicking your feet out. Come back to the others, rejoining hands and walk two paces to the left, then shuffle kick your feet forward three times. Step left twice and then right once and then dance in a small circle kicking your feet out again.*

"It goes by many names, but I call it the *Branle de Bourgogne*," he answered.

Soon I got the hang of it. Every time I danced in my own little circle I couldn't help but laugh and smile. It was the first real bit of fun I'd had in a really long time. Ares was smiling too, his perfect, true smile and the sight of him dancing and spinning happily with me made me happier than a hundred dead rabbits could.

"I have to say I'm surprised you're such a good dancer," I admitted as we continued the dance.

Ares smiled. "It is but one of the many surprises about me that you will soon learn. You have to remember that I have been alive a *very* long time, Sunshine."

As we neared the band, he cleared his throat. The band leader nodded and the traditional song changed to one song I remembered from my high school days. Ares pressed me close against him and began to grind his body into mine. I had seen my fellow classmates dance like this, but I had never done it, or experienced it. Ares moved behind me and helped me move my hips along with the beat and his movements.

I could feel Achilles' anger skyrocket as I reached back and wrapped an arm around Ares' neck, pressing us even closer together. I didn't want him to be mad, but at the same time I knew Ares was doing this for me. I deserved something for me.

Ares and I danced until the song ended and then he bowed to me, holding my hand and kissing the back of it softly. "Thank you for the dances."

I curtsied and said, "It was an honor to dance with the great Prince of the Sidhe and Werewolves."

He stood up and hugged me tightly. "You're too perfect for me."

I laughed and shook my head. "I am definitely not perfect. You, sir, are too good for me."

He nipped my ear playfully. "I could be bad if you wanted me to."

Achilles cleared his throat and we both turned to smile at him. "Did you enjoy your dances?"

I grinned. "I did. You're both incredible dancers! I never thought about you both knowing how to ballroom dance before."

"Perhaps you would like to dance with the man who invented ballroom dancing then," said Zeus from behind me.

I turned around and curtsied. "It would be a great pleasure for me to dance with the King of the Sidhe."

He picked my hand up and kissed my fingertips softly. "The pleasure is all mine, my dear." He winked at me and then spun me away from his two sons and back onto the dance floor. The song was slow, luckily, and Zeus led us in a simple box step. "I see there is still tension amongst you three."

I sighed. "Yes, but I don't see how to fix it. Achilles is upset because he wants me to mate with him, but Ares doesn't want that. I don't want to upset Ares, yet I do feel the draw to Achilles. But every time I start kissing Achilles I feel like I'm betraying Ares." I groaned and leaned my forehead against his shoulder. "What do I do?"

Zeus patted me on the back and then hugged me. "You need to make the decision that is right to you. I love both of my sons and want to see them happy, but I'm not going to tell you to do something that you might regret or that will make you uncomfortable. Give it time, dear. You've only been back with us for a short while. There is no need to rush things."

"Thank you. May we take a break? I would love to keep dancing, but I'm tired."

Zeus bowed to me and led me back to Ares and Achilles. "I return your beloved to you and thank you for allowing this old man to dance with such a beautiful woman." He leaned close to me and whispered, "Good luck."

I frowned at him and watched as he walked away laughing.

"What was that about?" Achilles asked.

"Just some fatherly talk from Zeus, nothing that needs to be discussed. I think I need a glass of water."

Ares and Achilles looked at each other a moment, communicating in that strange silent guy way and then they both ushered me back to our table. I sat down and accepted the glass of water Achilles handed to me. I hadn't noticed until I'd said something, but I was incredibly thirsty and a little lightheaded.

"You should have told me you were lightheaded," said Ares softly.

I shook my head. "I wasn't until I told you I needed a glass of water."

A Sidhe woman with green colored skin knelt before me. "May I assess your health, Princess? I am a healer."

I looked at Ares who nodded. "Sure," I said, "But I don't think it's necessary. I just got a little dehydrated."

She smiled sweetly at me and placed one hand on my stomach and one hand on the center of my chest. She was silent for four of my heartbeats and then pulled her hands away. "You're in very good health. Drink plenty of water and stay away from alcohol since it dehydrates." She stood up and turned to Achilles, motioning for him to follow her. He obeyed and they talked a few yards away.

Ares stroked my cheek. "How are you feeling?"

"I feel fine, Ares. I didn't mean to startle you both."

Suddenly, a pain flashed through me. Achilles' anger was like a whip of fire against my skin. I gasped and turned to face him. He stood alone where he and the healer had been talking a moment ago. Why was he so angry all of a sudden? His back was to me, making it impossible to gauge his problem from his face.

"What's wrong?" Ares asked.

"Achilles is very angry," I whispered.

Achilles straightened and turned to us, a smile on his face. "Sorry, Artemis. I saw someone I did not wish to. How are you feeling?"

He was pretending as though he wasn't mad, but I could feel the anger and pain simmering beneath his smile. His eyes were also pinched, a sign of pain. "I'm fine. How are you? Why are you in pain?"

He sighed, looked down at his feet and then laughed. "This bond is burdensome in a few areas. I'm fine, just dealing with feelings about something I cannot deal with. You needn't worry, you have done nothing and I am not mad at you." He reached down and patted my hand reassuringly.

Why were men so stubborn? Why did they have to be hard asses all the time?

WE RETURNED to Hera's court and the rest of our pack to find a hundred Sidhe dressed in battle armor and practicing with swords, bows, and axes. Our pack watched from the sidelines, but I could see them taking it all in as they tried to memorize the moves.

Koda waved at us from the front where he was practicing using a bow and arrow with Erebos. I jogged over to him and asked, "Can I try?"

Erebos handed me a wooden bow instead of the silver one he had been using. I nocked an arrow, aimed and released. The solid "thunk" of the arrow hitting the target brought a smile to my face even before I saw that I'd hit the very center of the bulls-eye.

Erebos whistled. "Wow. You are definitely a natural with a bow." He turned and yelled, "Hephaistos!"

The tall Sidhe with forearms as big as my legs jogged up to us. "Yes?"

Erebos pointed to me. "You remember Artemis, right?"

Hephaistos dropped to one knee and bowed his head. "Princess."

I still wasn't used to this type of treatment, especially not after pretending to be human for so long. "Stand, please."

He stood and looked at Erebos who said, "She's a natural, as you can see."

Hephaistos smiled. "Indeed, she is."

"I would be greatly appreciative and honored if you would make me a bow and set of arrows. Your brand was great," I said.

He bowed. "Thank you. I'll return as soon as it's finished."

I spun around and jogged to find Ares. "Ares!"

He turned from his discussion with a pack member and met eyes with me. "What's wrong?"

"What happened to the humans? All those people we gave the brand to? I completely forgot to ask with all of this mayhem going on."

He averted his eyes a moment and said, "That's something we should discuss later."

"Why? What happened?" I asked frantically. "Where are the townspeople and all of the other humans from everywhere that we went? What happened to them?" Everyone had stopped practicing and turned towards me, but I didn't care. I had to know what happened.

Ares took my hands in his. "I'm sorry, Artemis. We were locked up so we couldn't help them. It's all my fault and I know it doesn't make it any easier, but…"

"They're all dead, aren't they?" I asked in a small voice.

He wrapped his arms around me and held me tightly against him, offering me his warmth and touch as my mate and pack mate to soothe me. "Yes. I'm sorry. Even if they hadn't been turned, humans don't live over one hundred years often."

Every person I'd grown up with in the town. Every person

who had believed in me and wanted to be saved from the preternaturals. They were all dead and it was my fault. I knew that I should be sad, that tears should be pouring from my eyes, but the only thing I felt was anger.

I pulled away from Ares and saw my glowing body reflected in his eyes. "The vampires killed them?"

Victor walked over to me from the castle. "Yes, my father had anyone bearing Ares' marked killed."

"When is the battle?" I asked through clenched teeth as I tried to reign in my anger and power.

"We leave in the morning," Victor said softly.

I inhaled deeply and shoved the anger and power down. I could open it up and use it tomorrow. I noticed that everyone was still staring at me, so I turned away and walked towards the other side of town. With the anger pushed away, my grieving surfaced. Tears streamed down my face and body. Wrenching sobs forced me to stop and sit down as I cried over the losses. People had died because they trusted me. They might have lived if I hadn't come to them. If the vampires had come and given them the choices, they might have chosen differently and been allowed to live, albeit as slaves. My head and body hurt from the fierce sobs breaking out of me. How could I save the world from the vampires when I had doomed hundreds or thousands or however many people to death already?

"Artemis, it's not your fault," said Achilles softly from beside me.

There was no way I could defeat the vampires. I was just a worthless girl on a power high. I should have given myself to Maurice before Hera had stolen me. Then everyone would be safe.

Achilles squatted down in front of me and grabbed my arms. His body was glowing and his eyes were solid white pearls as he looked into my eyes. "You listen to me! Giving yourself to Maurice would not have accomplished anything except your torture and possibly our deaths as we tried to rescue you. Do not ever think about giving yourself to that monster! I would sooner give up my life than see you in his hands."

"If you died I would die too," I whispered softly as I wiped at the tear tracks on my face.

Achilles stopped glowing and the warm gentleness returned to his eyes. "Yes, I know. I was just trying to make a point." He sat down beside me and I let him take me into his arms. "It was not your fault. It was Maurice's decree and his vampires who executed them. The only person you should be mad at is Maurice."

He was right, but it didn't help the pain I felt in my heart. Inside it felt as though I had stamped their execution orders with my brand.

He rubbed his hands up and down my arms and started to sing in a language I didn't understand. His voice was amazing and the language was incredibly beautiful. We sat together for at least an hour and he didn't stop singing until Ares approached us.

Ares sat down and picked my hand up in his. I expected him to be angry that I had run off and he had found me with Achilles, but he did the most unexpected thing. He started singing where Achilles had left off. Achilles joined Ares and the brothers sang to me while the grief and sorrow I felt eased and then settled into a low ache.

They stopped singing when they determined I was no longer in pain and cuddled around me from both sides as comfort. Ares kissed my cheek and stood up. "I'll be on the training field when you're ready to return."

"Ares," I whispered. He looked at me and the sadness in his eyes made me struggle for a moment. "Thank you," I finally managed to say.

He dipped his head and disappeared around the corner of a building.

Achilles stroked my hair and whispered, "I love you, Artemis. I'm sorry that things are so difficult for you. If there is anything I can do to make it easier, please tell me."

"You've done so much already, Achilles. More than I could have hoped for."

He adjusted our position so that I was leaning against his chest and hugged me tight. "Will you please stay beside me during the fight tomorrow? I know you don't like the idea of us guarding you, but if it were up to me I would leave you behind for the fight. After you were gone so long, we've had so little time to spend with you."

"My life always seems to be hectic. We rush from one fight to another or one place to another. I just want this war to be over and the world to return to what it was, or as close as it can be."

"Will you stay by me?" he asked again.

I nodded and turned to face him. "Yes, but you have to focus on yourself and not me. If I get into trouble I can always use the sunlight magic."

Achilles smiled. "I will try to remember that." His smile wilted a moment and then he kissed me on the lips. Unlike Ares' kisses which filled me with a raging fire, Achilles' kiss filled me with an electric buzz, as if I was holding a live wire.

His hands ran from my shoulders to my stomach to my back and then he pulled me closer to him. It felt wrong to be kissing someone other than Ares and yet it also felt so incredibly right to kiss Achilles.

He pulled away first, and I knew without looking that both of our wings were out and that my eyes were pearl white like his. He smiled one of the first true smiles I had ever seen on his face, and yet I could sense sadness in him as well. He kissed my lips quickly. "Come on, we should get back. I'm sure Hephaistos has your bow ready."

I let him help me stand. It took a moment of intense concentration for me to calm my powers and bring my wings in. I was suddenly glad that he'd pulled back since I hadn't.

We walked back to the field where everyone, halfbreed and Sidhe, were now practicing together. It warmed my heart more than a million kisses could. Koda put his arm around my shoulders and pulled me away from Achilles and towards Hephaistos and Erebos. "You have to see what Hephaistos worked up for you."

"Sweet," I said excitedly as we increased our speed to get to Hephaistos.

Hephaistos smiled at me and then blushed. "I got a bit carried away, but I think you'll like what I've made."

I smiled at him. "I'm sure I'll love it. Your work is always beautiful."

He picked up a covered bundle from the table behind him and slowly unwrapped it, revealing a beautiful bow. Never before had I seen one so exquisitely crafted. The frame was covered in intricate carvings of vines which matched the ones on my face and arms. The string and frame were both a glowing silver color and seemed to throb as though alive. "I made sure not to use any silver since I know you're allergic to it, but I couldn't make you a bow simply out of wood."

Achilles and Ares had joined us and at the sight of the bow in Hephaistos' hands they both gasped. Achilles asked, "How long has it been since you made a bow this way?"

Hephaistos smiled. "Too long, but I believe Princess Artemis is the best recipient for such an item."

I cleared my throat and they all turned to me. "May I see the bow to understand why you are all so excited?"

Hephaistos laughed and held out the bow. "My apologies."

The bow was much lighter than I expected and as soon as it touched my skin I understood the excitement. My back arched in a mixture of pain and pleasure as the bow determined if I were suitable to hold it or not. After a moment the power of the bow receded and it vibrated slightly in my hand. "How did you harness starlight to keep the form of the bow?" I asked in shock.

"We are Children of the Stars and a mother is always willing to help her children," Hephaistos answered softly. "I am glad that you are able to wield it. I had not thought about the possibility of you being unable to."

I laughed and pulled on the string which was also made from starlight to test its resistance. "Do you have an arrow I can try?"

Hephaistos unwrapped another bundle and I gasped. "Starlight arrows?"

He smiled. "Starlight shafts with steel tips which have been dipped in sunlight."

Several of the crowd which had gathered gasped and started talking loudly.

I picked up one of the arrows and nocked it. I looked across the field and saw a target about two miles away. I aimed and released. The arrow sped across the field faster than any normal silver or wood arrow could and flew through the target and into the tree behind it.

"I never knew you were an archer," Ares said teasingly.

I shrugged. "It appears so."

I ran to the tree and pulled the arrow from the trunk. The tip of the arrow was no longer dipped in sunlight. I jogged back to the group, slung my bow over my shoulder and formed a ball of sunlight in my palm. I dipped the tip of the arrowhead in the sunlight and turned it slowly so that the sunlight coated it. "How does it stick?" I asked Hephaistos as I coated the arrow head.

"The iron is enchanted and the starlight can understand your desire and assists as best as it can," he said in an awed whisper.

I put the arrow back into the sheath and looked up at all of the eyes focused on me. "What?" I asked as I blushed.

"I was not aware that you could control sunlight," said Erebos from beside me.

I smiled at him. "Yes, I can."

"Ares!" Koda called. "We have a problem."

I followed Ares over to where Koda was standing with an unfamiliar Sidhe on the other side of the grass. The Sidhe left and Koda kept looking at me in a weird way, almost as if he was uncomfortable with me being there. "What's wrong?" asked Ares.

Koda looked at me a moment then sighed. "You'll find out anyways so I might as well just tell him in front of you. Ares, they're fighting a werewolf in the Games."

Ares folded his arms across his chest and it took me a moment to stop staring at his biceps. "Why is that a problem?" Ares asked. "They've used a wolf before to fight one of the humans."

"It's a problem because the wolf isn't fighting a human. The wolf is fighting an elf," Koda said slowly as though trying to clue Ares into the secret without letting me figure it out. I really wished I could read his mind. Where was Victor when you needed him?

Ares asked, "What did the wolf do? Which wolf is it?"

"The wolf killed a vampire to protect a human that did not have his brand." Koda stopped talking, looking at me for a long moment before saying, "It's Bret."

"My Bret?" I asked in shock. Ares growled and I rolled my eyes at him. "You know I didn't mean it like that."

Koda smiled at me. "Yes, your Bret."

Ares sighed. "Crap."

"What are the Games?" I asked.

"They're like the old Roman gladiator fights to the death, but usually the humans are pitted against ogres or some other preternatural. It's rare that a preternatural has to fight another preternatural, but in some instances, they do it. Usually the fight serves as a public execution."

"And Bret is going to have to fight in it?" Dread overwhelmed me.. I turned to Ares. "We have to save him. We can't just let him die, especially if he was protecting a human."

Ares closed his eyes and rubbed his temples with his fingers, as though trying to get rid of a headache. "I knew you were going to say that," he whispered.

"That's why I didn't want to tell you in front of her," said Koda.

"Where're the Games held? How long will it take to get there? When is he fighting?" I asked frantically.

Ares threaded his fingers through mine, giving me reassurance and calming me. "Koda and I will take care of it. You stay here with Achilles."

"No way!" I yelled, pulling my hand from his. "You're not leaving me behind."

"Artemis, the stands are going to be full of vampires and

Maurice will be there, sitting in the pulpit, watching over everything. Do you really think it's a good idea for you to go?"

"You're not leaving me behind. I'll teleport myself to the Games if you try to leave me." I was not giving up on this. No matter what he said I was going.

"She'd probably teleport herself right into the center of the ring," said Koda more to himself than anyone else.

Ares growled. "I am not taking you there! What if Maurice catches you?"

"I'll teleport out," I answered quickly.

"She has a point," said Koda.

Achilles walked towards us, a deep frown on his face. "What's going on?" He must have sensed my anger and come looking for me.

"Artemis' former friend is being fought in the Games. She wants to go with us and threatened to teleport herself if we leave her behind," summarized Koda.

Achilles gaped. "You can't go to the Games. It's not really even safe for Ares to go to the Games. What if you get captured?"

"I'll teleport out," I said calmly.

"It's not that simple," Achilles said with a hiss, "They could kill you before you had a chance to teleport. And we all know that you wouldn't leave us behind just to save yourself. You are not going, Artemis."

My mouth dropped open. Achilles had never spoken to me that way before. I expected it from Ares, but not Achilles. "You don't make the decisions for me," I said quietly trying to summon my anger, but in my shock I was unable.

"I am your mate, whether we've *mated* or not and therefore I do have a say in what you do, especially if it puts your life, and consequently mine, at risk. Plus, you're the Princess of the Sidhe and it's every Sidhe's job to protect you. Do you really want to fight off the entire Sidhe race just to go rescue Bret?"

Never in my life would I have expected Achilles to speak to me like this. "You're trying to push me into a corner."

He smiled. "No, sweetheart, I shoved you into the corner and shackled you there. Ares, Koda and I will go to the Games and save your friend. You will stay here, watched by Sidhe guards whom I know you won't hurt and you will wait for us to return. Are we clear?"

I turned to Ares. "He can't really do this, can he?"

Ares smiled sympathetically. "He just did."

Erebos, Heracles and Theseus walked towards us from the training ring where they'd been sparing. Without a word, Erebos grabbed hold of my left arm and Theseus grabbed my right and together they held me in place.

"Let me go!" I yelled as I struggled against them.

Ares said, "Maybe we should get Hades?"

Achilles smiled. "That's a much better plan. Hades!"

"What are you going to do, have him kill me?" I asked angrily.

Ares, Achilles and Koda all rolled their eyes at me at the same time. Ares stepped forward and kissed my forehead softly. "We'll be back as soon as we can."

Koda kissed my cheek and then Achilles stepped in front of me. "I don't like doing this to you, Artemis, but your safety is my top concern. I can't lose you again." There was such pain in his voice that it made my heart ache and made me wish to touch him and console him. Unfortunately, I was being held against my will so I found the strength to refrain.

"Achilles, please let me come with you. I can help you. I

don't want to be sitting here on my hands fretting and wondering if you're okay or not."

He smiled and kissed my lips softly, sending a pleasant shock through my body. "You won't have to."

Hades stepped forward and smiled at me. "Hello, Princess. This won't hurt, but you're going to feel a little woozy."

"Ares! Achilles!" I called to them as they walked away from me. Neither man turned back around towards me. I felt my heart hammering against my chest as they walked away and my hands started shaking. I didn't want to be away from them. I didn't want separation. Hades pressed his hand to my forehead and chanted a few words in a strange language. I struggled against Theseus and Erebos, but my limbs were growing heavy and my eyelids were becoming increasingly hard to keep open. "This. Is. Cheating," I panted out just before Hades' spell slipped me into sleep.

The look on her face tore at my heart. I hated forcing her to stay behind, but I could not bear to see her get hurt. Her indignant feelings would mend when we returned, but her death would ruin us all. Especially since if she died, I would. If we died, I wouldn't even be able to grieve for her, which would eat at my soul for eternity.

"You did the right thing, Achilles. I'm actually very surprised and proud of you," said Ares as we headed towards the main building and my mother's quarters.

"I know I did the right thing. I just can't stand the look she gave me. She feels as though I've betrayed her."

Part of me was still angry at Ares for what I'd learned from the healer, but I didn't want to tell him yet. I'd tell him soon, but not yet. And for now, I dismissed the anger and focused on the task at hand.

"She's only worried for your safety. She'll be asleep so she won't even have time to fret," said Koda. "Besides, she knows you only did it to keep her safe. She'll forgive you."

I wasn't so sure. She may forgive me, but that didn't mean

she'd trust me again or look at me the same. I already missed the smell of her skin, the touch of her hand.

"You think Hera will be in a good mood?" Ares asked as we entered the building and headed down the left corridor towards her room. The paintings on the wall became progressively darker with scenes shifting from peaceful meadows to a stormy sea to a bloody war. They were the visual progression of my mother's moods when she was displeased, or at least that's what I thought.

"I doubt it, but she owes us much for the past one hundred years," I answered quietly as I knocked on the door.

"Enter," exclaimed my mother in her most regal voice.

I pushed open her door and found my mother, the Queen of the Sidhe, in a fluffy pink bathrobe sitting in a chair with maids painting her fingernails and toenails. "Achilles!" she said happily. "To what do I owe this visit?"

"We need your help," I said blinking at her. "We need to rescue someone from the Games and bring them back."

She stood up and all of her maids backed away. "A Sidhe is in the Games?" she asked, her lips thin.

I shook my head. "No, it's a werewolf, one who used to be a friend of Artemis'."

"Where is our favorite halfbreed?" she asked as she examined her fingernails, no longer worried now that she knew it wasn't a Sidhe in the Games.

"Hades put her to sleep because she was refusing to stay behind and threatening to teleport if we left without her," Koda explained.

Hera smiled. "She's very feisty."

Ares scoffed. "That's an understatement."

"What is it that you need from me?" she asked as she sat

back down in her chair and let the maids resume pampering her.

"We need you to teleport us to and from the Games," I said as I plucked a grape from a dish on the table beside me and popped it into my mouth. The grape was perfectly ripe and extremely juicy. Of course, the Queen of the Sidhe demanded the best.

Hera sighed. "I was afraid you were going to say that. Very well, let me get changed and I'll teleport you all."

Ares, Koda and I walked out of her room and leaned against the wall in the hallway. "What's your plan for when we arrive?" I asked Ares.

He shrugged. "Find where they have him, take him."

"That's not a very well thought out plan," I said incredulously.

He smiled. "I'll figure something out. I always do."

I lifted a brow. "Like the time we stole Dad's Pegasus to race him against the elves and started a war?"

Ares smiled. "You're the one who called the elf names and started it all. I only gave you a way to end it. It's not my fault that my spear accidentally fell while we were racing and tripped their steed."

I shook my head and laughed. "Right. And it wasn't your fault that the elves' shields all disintegrated during the war either."

"I can neither confirm nor deny if that acid was from my personal stores or not," Ares said in a monotonous tone.

I laughed and then sighed. "That battle lasted five years. Father was furious with us."

"But, who won? We did, because elves are awful at battle strategizing."

"And because you pull crazy schemes out of your butt and they actually work," Koda said as he leaned against the wall.

Ares smiled. "You're both just jealous because I'm the God of War."

"Conceited," I whispered.

"Vain," Koda whispered at the same time.

Hera stepped out of her room and frowned at me. "I hope you aren't talking about me."

I smiled. "Of course not! I would never speak of my lovely mother in such a manner."

She didn't seem convinced, but she left it alone. "Ready?"

We all reached a hand out and touched her shoulders. "Try not to land us in the center of the arena, please," Ares said.

She sighed. "So little faith. I will transport us in the back area where they keep those to be fought."

She closed her eyes and sent us whirling through the vortex of teleportation. I hated the feeling more than anything else, preferring even to have a sword cut me than to spin around and around.

"You can open your eyes now," she whispered.

I opened them and found us in an underground room with stone walls, dirt floors, and a metal gate. "You teleported us to a prisoner's cell? How did you know to come here? When were you in a prisoner's cell?" I asked.

"There are many things that you don't know about me and many more things that I will never tell you. Just be happy that I had knowledge of this place and could get us here. Otherwise, we would be trying to walk through the front door." She pushed open the cell door and marched down the aisles of cells as though she owned the place. Ares and Koda searched each prisoner's face as we wound our way through the holding area, but they did not find who they were looking for.

The crowd roared above us and dirt sifted from the ceiling down onto us. "Perhaps he is already fighting," I suggested.

Ares sighed. "I did not want to go out into the arena."

Hera grabbed a guard who had been watching the fight through an iron fence. "Who fights right now?" she asked him as she pressed him up against the fence.

"A werewolf and elf."

She smiled and grabbed his keys from his belt. "Thank you."

She opened the gate and turned to Ares. "We run out, grab him and teleport, got it?"

Ares smiled. "Sounds like a plan to me."

We stepped out into the arena, and I nearly choked. Bret wasn't just fighting one elf, he was fighting six. His sides were smeared with blood and his chest was heaving as he gasped for breath. The six elves stood around him in a loose circle holding spears.

The crowd was roaring, but then all eyes turned to us and they silenced. Maurice stood from his seat in the **pulpit**, smiling down at us. "I've been waiting for you." He turned to the crowd and said, "It seems we have additional fighters." He looked at our group a moment and then frowned. He was probably annoyed that Artemis wasn't with us. For once we did not let her endanger herself, and her hurt feelings no longer bothered me.

The crowd took a moment to understand the shift in the situation, but then they cheered in anticipation of bloodshed. I looked around the stands and was surprised to see beings from every race, *including Sidhe*, attending the Games.

Ares turned and smiled at me. "I'd always dreamed of fighting in the Arena, but father wouldn't allow me to in the Roman days. That's why I owned that group of gladiators and trained them instead of fighting. Oh, Spartacus, that was one hell of a gladiator. I do wish he had let me turn him." He stopped his reminiscing and looked at the elves. "You think the elves remember me?" He ripped his shirt off and took a half shift, growling at the crowd, sounding more like a lion than a wolf.

The elves turned and fixed their gazes on him. Yep, they remembered him. Ares charged forward, slicing one of the elves' heads almost completely off with his claws. Bret limped towards Ares, clutching his side and a wound which was dripping onto the sand.

The cool night air caressed my skin as I took a step forward. Small glass balls enchanted with a light spell sat in little holders around the arena and throughout the stands so the attendees could see everything even though it was night time. The smell and feel of the sand at my feet and the roar of the crowd brought back many memories of my younger days in Rome. Of course, back then I'd been revered as a god, sitting in the pulpit, watching, and determining the fates of the gladiators, not participating. Like Ares I had always wanted to participate, but father had forbidden us from fighting. I looked around at the eons old architecture and wished Artemis was here, knowing she would have enjoyed seeing the coliseum. Although it was not nearly as spectacular now as it was in its original days. I did have to admit that it was nice to be able to look in the stands without finding couples fornicating though. Romans were such vile creatures.

I turned back to the issue at hand and ran forward, releasing my powers, but not my wings and used a fireball to push back the elves. Koda ran at my side, now in wolf form and snapped his teeth at them.

Hera walked behind us at a leisurely pace as though we were simply walking through a park.

"What are you doing here?" asked Bret with more growl to his voice than human words.

"Saving you," Ares said. "Now shut up and go stand by the Sidhe Queen."

Bret looked like he wanted to object, but he limped his way to Hera and stood beside her. "I hope you know what you're doing," he whispered.

I came over to stand beside Ares and smiled at the elves. "It's been so long since I've seen elves bleed. I should like to draw this fight out a bit."

Ares laughed, sounding incredibly creepy in his half shift. "The crowd craves blood, let's give them a show!"

The elves charged forward, their eyes burning with blood lust. I dodged the spear one threw at me and kicked him in the chest, making him fly backwards to land on his back. An elf charged at Ares, but Ares snapped the spear in half and then impaled the elf with the end he'd broken off.

The crowd cheered madly, standing up and raising their fists in the air. Koda walked backwards and sat beside Bret, apparently deciding that we didn't need help in this fight.

The elf I'd kicked jumped up and flung dirt at my face. I covered my face, but he punched me in the ribs, knocking my breath from me. "Dirty little elf!" I yelled as I backhanded him across the face and then kicked his legs out from under him. I dropped down onto his body and began punching his face as hard and as fast as I could. Blood sprayed and it took me a minute to realize that he was dead. I stood up and walked to stand beside Ares. I had a moment to feel excited that I was standing beside my brother again in battle, before refocusing on the situation.

Two of the elves charged at us, so we grabbed them both in headlocks and snapped their heads off simultaneously. That maneuver pleased the crowd who were all on their feet, screaming themselves hoarse.

Ares and I looked at the final elf who now seemed scared. "How should we kill this one?" Ares asked as he began pacing in a wide circle around the elf. "The crowd wants a messy death. They want someone ripped in two."

"Or perhaps sliced up into multiple pieces," I suggested, "we did end this fight too quickly."

Ares ripped the spear from the body of the elf he'd killed. "That is a good suggestion, but I think beheading him might be the most pleasing to the crowd. Plus, I grow bored with these Games."

Ares spun around and sliced the elf's head clean off. The elf's body fell to the ground twitching and Ares stabbed the spear into the bottom of the head, holding it up above him and then flung it into the crowd.

Maurice raised his hand and four men blew on their trumpets. A gate to the left of us opened and the crowd grew silent in anticipation.

"What do you suppose he's kept hidden from us?" I asked as I stood beside Ares, watching the gate.

"It would have to be something extremely powerful to take out both of us," Ares said with a somewhat demented smile on his half wolf-half man face. "I hope its ogres."

The trumpets blew again and a spear flew from the darkness of the gate. Ares and I dodged separate ways, avoiding the spear by mere inches. The spear imbedded into the stone wall behind us. I turned and inspected the spear, knowing Ares would warn me of any attacks. "It's embedded over two feet. Something strong is waiting for us."

Ares scoffed. "I could have embedded it five feet at least, with your body hanging from it."

Standing beside him once more, I stared into the open gate. "You think it's a machine? A preternatural should have come out by now instead of cowering in there like a scared whelp."

A roar quite similar to Ares' sounded and then a werewolf in half shift walked out of the shadows.

Ares growled. "Darius. I should have known since he was always awful at all of the sporting contests we held in Lyngvi every century."

"Why would your King fight in the Games against you?" I asked. Such a thing would never happen among the Sidhe.

"He thinks he can best me and wants it to be public. He will soon learn the error of his ways."

"Why would Darren and Darius betray their own race?" I still could not understand it.

Ares smiled. "Because they think Maurice is stronger than he really is. They don't realize how strong Victor is since he's been hiding it and only lets me see his true power. In order to keep from being overtaken, the two cowardly wolves bowed to the Vampire King to save their own hides. That's why Darren betrayed his own daughter and the wolves. They're scum and I plan to kill Darius now so the pack is clean of his cowardice."

Darius stopped once he'd reached the center of the ring and then tilted his head back and howled. Six wolves ran out of the gate to stand behind him, all snarling and frothing at the mouth.

"He brought some pups with him," Ares said with a smile on his face. "It has been a long time since I've fought my own kind."

"Ares," I whispered, moving closer to him, "Won't you be unable to move against him if he commands you since he's your alpha?"

Ares laughed. "That fool has never been my alpha. He knows that I am the true alpha of the werewolves and that's why he can't even fight me on his own. I should have killed that bitch years ago, but my mother had seemed happy with him." He frowned a moment and then said, "I hope she likes being a widow."

Maurice raised his arms and the chattering of the crowd stopped. "Today we have a rare feast for you. Today the Alpha of the Werewolves fights the Beta of the Werewolves in a fight to the death!"

"I've grown tired of your annoying presence," Darius said to Ares. "I only wish your halfbreed bitch was here so I could kill her too."

Ares growled loudly. "You've done nothing, but sully the name of Werewolves. I intend to fix that presently. Once I've killed you and ripped your heart from your body, I will take my true position as Alpha and see that we are restored to our original place of honor. No longer shall we be second to the vampires, but soon we will be their equals as we should be!"

Ares sprinted forward, slashing and punching at Darius so fast that it was hard for even *my* eyes to track. The other wolves started to move towards Ares, but I ran forward, cutting them off, forming a wall of fire between me and them. Koda ran from his spot beside my mother to jump on the back of the nearest wolf. He bit into the scruff of the wolf and shook his head fast. The wolf struggled against Koda, but with one more quick shake he snapped the wolf's neck and released his hold to let the dead body fall to the ground. The other wolves turned and growled at Koda. He shifted to his human form and said, "Submit or die!"

The wolves' knees trembled as they fought against his command. Being third in the werewolf hierarchy made Koda's commands very difficult to ignore. I released my wall of fire and turned to see how Ares was faring.

Ares' left arm bled from three cuts he must have received from Darius' claws. Darius was the worse for wear as he had cuts littering his body and a pool of blood forming at his feet in the sand. Both were fighting fiercely however, so Darius wasn't hurt enough to be slowed down.

I saw movement out of the corner of my eye and turned just as one of the wolves jumped at me. He knocked me to the ground, snapping his jaw at my throat. I shoved him off and stood up. "Thanks for the warning, Koda," I said as I looked for him.

"Sorry, I sort of have my hands full and didn't see that one slip away," he said where he was sitting on top of a pile of five men all whining and whimpering.

I turned and grabbed the wolf by its throat as it charged at me again and held it up. "Charging madly will not win the fight. You must learn to be stealthy and silent."

I tossed him towards Koda who grabbed him and forced him to change back to man. "Lie down and be still like the rest of your brothers," commanded Koda.

I laughed and shook my head as the five men lay down and remained still. Perhaps Ares was not the only one capable of being Alpha. With the wolves taken care of, that only left Ares and Darius left to battle it out. I returned to Hera and sat down on the ground beside her. "How has the fight gone?"

"Darius has opened a few cuts and landed a few hits, whereas Ares has opened at least a hundred cuts and has landed as many hits. Unfortunately, Darius does not seem to be slowing or weakening." She closed her eyes a moment and then opened them to stare intently at Darius. "I wonder if there is some type of spell keeping him from feeling pain or from weakening. He should be slowing by now."

"I don't see anything," I said as I watched Darius and Ares exchanging blows.

She frowned. "It could be a talisman or a stone enchanted with the spell."

I watched as Ares and Darius fought and sighed. "I can't tell from so far away. Ares! He's got a talisman or stone that's keeping him from weakening! You have to get it away from him before you can defeat him, short of ripping his head off!"

Ares growled and slashed at Darius' throat, but Darius stepped back in the nick of time, missing Ares' claws. "Can't even fight me fairly, can you Darius?" Ares yelled as he attacked him. Darius swung at Ares, and Ares dropped to the ground, picking up a spear shaft. He swung the shaft into Darius' upper right leg and then into his left. Darius growled and tried to grab the shaft, but Ares swung it up, connecting with Darius' jaw and making him fly up into the air. Darius landed on his back on the ground and started to get up, but Ares straddled his chest, pinning his arms with his legs and shoving the shaft against his throat. Ares ripped a necklace off of Darius' neck and tossed it towards me. "Is that it?" he asked as he punched Darius' face again and again. Blood sprayed from Darius' nose as Ares broke it, but Darius just continued to struggle against Ares.

Hera took the necklace and shook her head. "Nope."

Ares spun around Darius in a wrestling move I'd often seen humans in the mixed martial arts competitions use and grabbed Darius' leg in a leg lock. He reached up with one hand while Darius struggled to free his leg and stuck it inside Darius' pocket. Darius yelled and tried to grab Ares' hand, but Ares held him down with his leg across his chest and tossed the stone to us before he could reach him.

Hera caught the stone and gasped. "Yes, this is it. You can kill him now."

Ares stood up off Darius who was now lying on the ground gasping in pain and moaning. "You thought you could defeat me with a cheap stone? A stupid spell! I could have just ripped your head off when I had you pinned on the ground, but that's too swift a death for you."

Darius shifted to his human form and whispered, "You're not wolf enough to be Alpha. They will not bow to you."

Ares laughed. "You can't even hold your form and you say *I'm* not wolf enough? I'm more wolf than you could ever hope to be!"

Ares kicked him in the ribs. "That is for frightening my mate." He grabbed Darius' arm and bent it backwards, breaking the bone. "That is for ordering me around the world on stupid missions simply because you couldn't stand seeing all of the females crawling all over me." He grabbed a spear and snapped off the tip. He sat down and with skill that suggested he'd done this many times before, cut open Darius' chest and tore his heart from it. "And that's for giving Matt's female to the vampires to assist in his treachery and death!"

The crowd exploded in cheers and began chanting, "Ares!" over and over again.

Ares threw the heart up into the pulpit at Maurice's feet. "A gift from the new Alpha of the Werewolves to the King of the Vampires. Don't say I never gave you anything."

Maurice glared at us from his seat. "You've won this time."

Ares smiled and touched his pointer finger to his forehead

in a mock salute. "We'll see you soon, Maurice."

We walked back to my mother, and she grabbed onto us, teleporting us back to the training ground. I looked down and sighed. "I'm covered in blood and dirt."

Ares shrugged, motioning to his own body. "I'm worse." He shifted back to full man and looked around expectantly. "Where would they have taken her?"

Bret dropped to his knees on the ground, winced, and grunted. "Thank you."

Ares pushed him on to his back and started examining his wounds. "You're welcome, but I didn't do it for you. I did it for Artemis. She would have been very upset if you were dead."

"Artemis? She's here?" Bret asked eyes widening, trying to stand up.

Ares pushed him back down. "Stay still. Yes, she's here, but she's sleeping. You need to lie still for about an hour for your wounds to heal properly."

"I need to get back. I need to find my people," Bret said as he tried to sit up again.

"Lie still!" Ares commanded. Bret stilled, unable to ignore Ares' command. "What people? Tell us how you got into the Games in the first place."

"I found the villagers from the town Artemis and I grew up in. They all had your brand, but they were living in the middle of nowhere on the run from vampires who had apparently tried to kill them. I've been protecting the descendants for the past hundred years."

Ares groaned. "Artemis is going to want to run out and find them when she hears of this."

"Do we have to tell her?" I asked.

Ares smiled. "As much as I would like to keep it from her,

we should tell her. Besides, Bret won't lie to her about it. Bret, we will wait until after tomorrow's battle to tell her though. I do not want to have her focus waver during the battle. Do you understand?"

Bret nodded. "Yes, Alpha."

"I'm going to clean up. Ares, you should probably do the same so Artemis doesn't faint when she sees you." I started for the main building where my quarters were.

"You don't think she would view it as sexy?" he asked as he stood up and flexed his biceps.

Koda laughed. "Artemis would if she had been in the battle with you, but since she was left behind she would only be worried."

Ares fingered his left arm where Darius had scratched him. "I hate when it's healing and it starts to itch. If you scratch it too hard you reopen it and it has to re-heal which then makes it itch again."

Koda smacked his hand. "This is why you have to suffer through it until it doesn't itch anymore."

"You'd be scratching it too if you were covered in dirt and blood and had cuts that were healing," Ares grumbled as he headed towards the main part of town where a public bath-house was run by Poseidon, a blue Sidhe who loved water.

I looked down at Bret who was still lying on the ground. "You can't move, can you?"

He shook his head. "I can't sit up at least."

"I'm going to wash up and change quickly and then I'll be back. Just relax and let your wounds heal."

"As if I can do anything else," Bret grumbled.

I ignored him and continued to my room. I really wished to soak in a bath, but I felt bad leaving Bret alone. I would feel much better once the blood and dirt was washed off my skin.

CHAPTER
TWENTY
ARTEMIS

My eyes opened slowly as I regained consciousness. I was surprised that I did not dream while I had been asleep, but being put in a spelled slumber was not the same as *falling* asleep. The room was dark, no lights anywhere. I sat up and was met with three pairs of eyes watching me from chairs in front of the bed. My night vision kicked in and as I looked around, I recognized my surroundings as Achilles' chambers. "Have they returned?" I asked nervously.

Theseus smiled. "They returned a few moments ago and are waiting for you in the training grounds. We are to escort you there."

"I've no need of an escort." I closed my eyes and focused on the image of the place I wanted to go and summoned my power.

Nothing happened.

"You cannot teleport while restrained in magical chains," said Erebos in his deep voice.

I opened my eyes and sighed. "Fine, escort me."

"You know we do not like doing this. We were ordered to guard you," said Heracles as he came to unchain me.

I sighed. "I know. I do not blame you or hold anger towards you."

Surrounded by the men who had been holding me prisoner, I now walked in a circle of protection. I knew that Ares and Achilles had forced me to stay behind to try to protect me and not having to wring my hands in worry had been good for my nerves, but I felt betrayed.

We walked through the halls of the main building of the Sidhe court and out through a set of large doors to the open grassy area used for training. Our pack of halfbreed wolves was all around Ares with eyes intently fixed on him. Ares looked up and smiled at me. There was something different about him. He seemed bigger somehow. I shook my head at the ridiculous thought. He couldn't have gotten bigger. So what was it?

The closer I got to him, the more I felt like bowing to him. That was a feeling I had not had in quite a long time around him. The pack made a path for me, but as I walked by, those nearest reached out to touch me. I smiled at them and held my hands out to touch some as I walked. The touch of the pack was even more reassuring than ever before. Had I changed somehow? Had Hades done something that permanently affected me?

I finally made it to Ares and looked over his body for marks. I couldn't see any, but then again, he was wearing a t-shirt and jeans. He leaned down and kissed me deeply, winding a hand through my hair and around my hips, pulling me against him. I melted into him and felt the fire building within me that Ares always ignited. He pulled back from the kiss and smiled at me. "Did you have a nice nap?"

"Yes." I wanted to be mad, but I couldn't even feign it while I was still high on the kiss. . I looked into his eyes and asked, "Why are you more, more wolf than normal? No, it's not that you're more wolf it's just that your aura is stronger. What changed?"

Ares said, "I've always been like this, but now that I've claimed my proper title it's more evident to you."

"Your proper title? What do you mean?" I asked, my nerves growing.

"I killed Darius. I'm the new Alpha of the Werewolves," he said with a wide grin.

"Alpha," said the pack behind us.

"You killed Darius! When? Where? How?" I asked. I stopped my questions and asked the question I should have asked first, "Did you save Bret?"

Ares grabbed my shoulders and turned me around. "See for yourself."

Bret stood from where he had been kneeling among the pack and walked slowly towards me. He stopped in front of me and smiled nervously. "Hey, Chicky."

Varying emotions warred with my mind, but I ignored all of them and threw my arms around his shoulders. Bret stiffened a moment and then wrapped his arms around me in a tight hug. We inhaled each other's scents, and I whispered his name. I pulled out of the hug and smiled at him. "I'm glad you're okay."

He picked up my hand and traced one of my vines. "You look even more beautiful than the last time I saw you."

I cringed, waiting for my power to release from his touch and my life to be even more chaotic and stressful than it was, but nothing happened. I exhaled in relief and heard Ares do the same behind me. "Thank you," I said softly.

Koda cleared his throat from beside us. I jumped, having not heard him walk up. I turned to him and hugged him. "Are you unhurt as well?"

He nodded as he hugged me. "I am. I also brought you a present."

"A present?" I asked as I stepped back from him.

Koda stepped to the left and motioned at the line of men who had been standing behind him. "Darius brought them to fight Ares, but I made them submit to me instead. They're our newest pack members and as Alpha Female I thought it appropriate that you meet them."

"Alpha Female?" I asked in shock. I turned to Ares. "What about your mom? Isn't she Alpha?"

Ares shook his head. "When a new Alpha male takes the position he either takes the former Alpha's mate to be his, or his current mate takes the position. Obviously, I'm not going to take my mom as a mate, so you're now Alpha Female of the Werewolves."

I was Alpha Female!

"Whoa," I said as I comprehended all that had happened. I turned to the wolves in line in front of me and walked so that I could see them all. Most appeared young looking and middle level in dominance. "Whom do you serve?" I asked them.

"The Alphas," they said together.

"Whom do you protect?" I asked as I walked down the line.

"The Alphas."

"Who am I?" I stopped in front of them at the center of their line.

"Artemis, Alpha Female."

I walked up to each man and inhaled his scent at his neck and rubbed my cheek against theirs to scent mark each as mine. Luckily being short let me do it without having to bend down at an awkward angle, though two of the men were so tall that I had to stand on tiptoe to reach their cheeks. When I'd finished I turned to the rest of the pack and said, "Embrace your new brothers."

The pack surged around the men and greeted them. Ares walked to me and wrapped his arms around my waist. "You did that very well."

"Thanks. I learned it from the real wolves. Well obviously not the talking part, but the rest," I said as I leaned back against him. I looked around and frowned. "Where's Achilles?"

"I'm here. I was just freshening up from our excursion."

I watched him walk up and felt my heart flutter. How could he affect me so? My reaction to Ares was different, but Achilles still raised my pulse and made my legs wobble. It wasn't right to be in love with two men at the same time and yet I was. Sometimes I really hated magic.

I pulled away from Ares and turned to face him and Achilles. "I wanted to show you something. I watched the dragons doing this and I'm pretty sure I can duplicate it, but I'd appreciate it if you two would stand nearby in case it gets out of my control."

Ares frowned and Achilles sighed and shook his head. I took that as an "okay".

I stepped out onto the field and waited until everyone else was off of the field and Ares and Achilles were relatively close. I closed my eyes. Selene had taught me to meditate to better control my powers, and I really hoped it worked now. Inhaling slowly and grounding myself with the earth around me and beneath my feet, I channeled my power to my hands. I raised them slowly up, heels of my palms touching while the rest of the palm turned up to create a funnel for the power. I pictured the one time I'd seen Blu perform this technique and opened my eyes as fire burst out of my palms in a swirling purple tornado. I focused on the energy of the element and lowered the swirling fire until it formed a solid, protective circle around me. With a deep breath, I ground my feet into the ground and the fire spread out, increasing its circumference until it surrounded the entire field. Sweat began to drip down my face as the pull of controlling the wild element strained my magical ability.

"Release it, Artemis!" yelled Ares.

I shook my head and slowly and painfully pulled it all back into me. With each foot of returned element my magic returned and my body refilled with energy.

"By the Mother of All, I have never seen something so incredible," whispered someone.

"She has to be the most powerful being on the planet," whispered another.

"No wonder halfbreeds were forbidden. We couldn't defeat her unless we used a large group of our top soldiers," whispered one of the Sidhe soldiers.

I pulled in the last bit and felt completely revitalized. I turned and smiled at Ares and Achilles. "I did it!"

Hera was standing behind them, having snuck up while I was testing the magic. She snarled and started glowing. I only had a second's notice to prepare as she shot fire at me from her palms. I formed a shield of fire around me and absorbed her shot at me. Those gathered now stared in terror at me instead of awe. Hera's eyes turned solid white as she drew on all of her power and increased the amount of fire directed at me, but my shield simply absorbed it. Ares started to move towards her, but she released her powers and stopped the fire.

Her body and eyes returned to normal, with fear in them. "Who taught you this magic?" she asked in a shocked whisper.

For a moment, I didn't want to tell her, but Ares bowed his head slightly to me, telling me it was okay. "The King of the Dragons taught me to create the fire shield and the other he had to use once to protect me," I answered. "A group of vampires found us in the woods together and ambushed us. One of them grabbed me by the throat before I could shift and in his anger, he used it."

Hera swallowed before asking, "Could you contact the dragons?"

I nodded. "Yes, if I needed to, but we won't need them tomorrow."

She shook her head. "I wasn't speaking about tomorrow."

I shrugged. "If we need them, I can contact Draco-Blu, but I don't know if they will help or not. They prefer to stay neutral."

Ares walked up to me and stared into my eyes. "How are you feeling?"

I smiled and kissed his lips. "I feel perfect. By drawing the element back into me, I replenish myself and thus have no loss and no negative side effects."

He smiled and put his arm around my shoulders. "That's quite a trick you've got there. Perhaps you should start teaching me to use some of my Sidhe powers."

I shook my head. "I think your father or brother should teach you that."

He laughed. "Right."

Hephaistos cleared his throat, drawing our attention to him. "I have something else for Princess Artemis as well."

Ares and I followed Hephaistos back to the table and I

noticed that the Sidhe backed away from us and made a path quicker than usual. Was I that powerful? Or that frightening?

Hephaistos stood in front of the table and blocked our view. "I took measurements by eye only so I hope it fights properly, but if not I can always remake them." He took a step to the side and there lay the most beautiful armor I'd ever seen.

I walked forward and gingerly touched the armor. "It's beautiful," I whispered, "I've never seen such incredible armor. Thank you."

Hephaistos bowed. "You are more than welcome, Princess."

I shook my head. "No, you can call me Artemis. Anyone who would go to such great lengths to create something as beautiful as this for me has to be a friend."

Hephaistos smiled. "Thank you, Artemis."

Ares asked, "Do you want to try it on?"

Of course I did, but I also didn't want to diminish the beauty of the armor by placing it against me.

Achilles groaned. "Really, Artemis? Here, let us help you put it on."

Ares looked at Achilles questioningly, and Achilles whispered into his ear. Ares groaned. "She'll never understand."

Achilles shook his head. "No, I don't think she will."

Before I could ask what they were talking about, they started lifting pieces of the armor and placing it on me. In a matter of seconds, I was dressed and, surprisingly, I didn't feel weighed down. I stretched and moved around to test the restrictions out. Ares held up his fists in the universal sign of "let's fight" and I threw a few punches and kicked at him a few times, all free of limitations. "Wow my movements aren't restricted at all and it's not any heavier than a sweater."

Hephaistos smiled. "Sidhe enchanted."

"It's great, Hephaistos. I love it."

He bowed. "I'm pleased you like it."

Ares and Achilles stripped me out of the armor and set it back on the table on top of the cloths it had been wrapped in. I yawned and Koda put his arm around my shoulders. "Tired, Darlin'?"

I nodded. "Yeah. It's been a busy week."

He led me away from the table and the group which had gathered. "Well, let's get you some food and then get you to bed. Tomorrow is a big morning."

I leaned my head against his shoulder and inhaled his scent. "It's good to be back with you again."

Koda smiled down at me. "It's good to have you back again. I missed you more than you'll ever know."

TWENTY-ONE

As the sun rose the next morning, the sounds of activity were already high as people prepared for battle. Ares, Koda, Achilles and I lay in the giant bed in Achilles' chambers staring up at the ceiling. I knew they were all worried for my safety and the possibility of losing me again. I was worried about the possibility of losing them and I admit, about the possibility of my prophesied death. Luckily, I had avoided the topic with Achilles and Ares, but it still bothered me. Even though I didn't know the date of my death, I knew others would die with me and that was what truly worried me. I had accepted my upcoming death, but I couldn't accept others dying with me.

Victor walked into the room and said, "It's time we all started to get ready."

Ares nodded, but instead of getting up, he rolled over and molded his body to my side. He whined softly and nuzzled my hair with his nose.

I rubbed his back with one arm while I held hands with

Achilles with the other. Koda lay at the bottom of the bed and snuggled my feet against his chest.

Victor sighed and then inhaled before he yelled, "Ares and Achilles! Quit acting like a couple of sniveling cowards! You've fought thousands of battles and this one will be no different! Now get up and get ready!"

Ares growled and stood up out of bed. "Damn pushy vampires."

Achilles sighed and climbed out of bed too, muttering to himself. Koda kissed the top of my foot and followed the other two men into the bathroom to prepare. I fluffed up my pillow and smiled at Victor. "You're nervous, aren't you?"

He sat on the edge of the bed facing me. "I have a bad feeling about today, but I'm not sure why."

"Where are we fighting?"

"France. Hera and you will have to teleport us all."

I finger combed my hair. "Okay, but I've never teleported from this realm to the human realm. Maybe we should use the portal and then once we're in the regular realm again I can teleport everyone."

Victor smiled. "Okay."

My stomach churned, and I clamped a hand over my mouth.

"Are you alright?" Victor asked with concern in his voice.

I shook my head and ran into the bathroom, shoving past the three men who were showering and brushing their teeth and made it to the toilet just in time.

Ares dropped to his knees beside me and pulled my hair back as I threw up everything in my stomach. "Artemis, what did you eat?"

I shook my head but couldn't talk as my stomach

constricted and I dry heaved. *Achilles, I didn't eat anything. I was just talking to Victor and had to run in here.*

Achilles relayed my thought to Ares, Koda and Victor, who had followed me into the bathroom. Achilles was acting off, distancing himself from me. Was he just worried about today? He hadn't spoken to me or Ares much last night, but he didn't seem mad either. He was blocking me so hard that the corners of his eyes were pinched from the strain.

"She's probably just worried about the battle," said Victor quietly.

I wanted to argue with him, but I *was* nervous. Finally, my stomach settled, and I could lean back. "He's probably right."

Ares helped me stand up and handed me a toothbrush. "If you notice anything abnormal, tell me right away. I don't want you going out on the battlefield if you're sick."

"I'm a freaking halfbreed. I thought we weren't supposed to get sick," I complained around my toothbrush.

"We're not, but you're also unique," Ares said as he ran his hand through his hair.

His bicep flexed and then relaxed as his arm moved. How was I so lucky that I snagged a guy with such a great body? He ran his other hand through his hair and I watched his bicep again.

All eyes turned to me and I realized that I'd moaned. "Sorry," I whispered as I resumed brushing my teeth, a blush on my cheeks.

Achilles climbed into the shower and turned the water on. His back was tense, but he relaxed after the water flowed over him a few minutes. Obviously, I wasn't the only one nervous.

Ares kissed my cheek and walked out of the bathroom. Koda laughed and I spit the water I had in my mouth at him.

He jumped out of the way and stuck his tongue out at me. "Missed."

Achilles pushed up the shower head and then used his powers to increase the flow of water to reach Koda, soaking the shirt he'd just put on. "I didn't."

Koda groaned. "You're not supposed to gang up on me. What happened to 'bros before hoes'?"

I finished putting my hair up into a ponytail, pointed at him and glared. "You better not have just called me what I think you did."

Koda raised his arms in surrender. "I was joking."

"And besides, which one are you?" I asked teasingly.

Koda's jaw dropped. "That's just mean."

I walked out of the bathroom and started putting on the armor that Hephaistos had designed for me. I slid the sheath of arrows onto my back and then draped the bow across my body diagonally until I needed it. Seeing all of the people I loved preparing for battle, preparing for their possible deaths, made me start to tear up. I walked back into the bathroom and wiped at my eyes before anyone could see me.

Ares rubbed my back reassuringly. "It's alright to be nervous."

I whispered, "Ares, if I lose you…"

He moved in one blink and had me wrapped in a hug against his body. "Don't think like that. I promise that we will not be separated. Not even death could keep us apart. *Verus amor vincit omnia.* Remember?"

I pressed my nose against his throat and inhaled his scent, drawing him in and holding the smell in for as long as I could. "I know. I love you, Ares."

"I love you too, Artemis Lupine."

I giggled and rested my head on his chest for a moment before pulling away from him. "I'm ready."

He slipped his fingers through mine and we walked back into the bedroom and ate. Once I started eating, the food stayed down and then we made our way out to the field where the portal to the human world existed. Hera, Zeus, our pack of halfbreeds and at least one hundred Sidhe stood waiting for us.

Everyone looked nervous and twitchy. One of the halfbreeds turned to talk to his neighbor, and I saw the brand on his arm, a crescent moon with a star. Ares and my brand. The anger I had shoved down the night before resurfaced and with it rose my powers. My body glowed bright, my wings popped out of my back and my vines sparkled.

I looked at the gathered warriors and said, "We are going to fight the vampires. I know some of you are fighting at the request of your king or alpha, but I want you to know *why* we are fighting. The vampires have turned the world which was filled with light and happiness into a world of darkness! A world where humans can't live freely. A world where Sidhe can't go out alone!" I paused to allow my words to sink in and then continued, my voice gaining momentum, "A world of hate and fear and misery. A world where the only important thing is feeding the vampires! They've killed millions of innocent people. They have killed my friends. They tried to kill me, which, in turn, would have killed Prince Achilles. They do not deserve to live. They are evil! They are darkness given form and it is our duty to kill them and right the balance!"

Everyone cheered and those with weapons raised them in the air. "When you go out on that battlefield, I don't want you to fight for your king or your alpha. I want you to fight for the rights of every race! I want you to fight for the return of humanity! I want you to fight for the return of the light!"

The warriors all cheered and then started filing through the portal to the human world. Ares smiled at me. "Nice speech."

I smiled at him and said, "Let's go kill some vampires."

Ares sighed dramatically, his hand against his forehead like a woman swooning over a man. "Isn't she dreamy?"

Zeus laughed. "Yes, son, she is definitely a perfect match for you."

I turned and headed into the portal, folding my wings close around my body as I walked up the staircase portal. We stepped out into the human world and I noticed that we had split into two groups, but they were mixed groups of half-breeds and Sidhe as opposed to a halfbreed group and a Sidhe group. Finally, we were making headway. Hera stood in the center of the first group so I walked to the next group and waited until the last person had walked out of the portal and the ground had closed up behind him.

"Ready?" I asked those gathered around me. Everyone placed a hand on each other so that we were all connected by touch. Hera nodded at me to express her readiness. "Try not to throw up on each other," I whispered just before I closed my eyes, and we spun through a spinning vortex. I opened my eyes and smiled at the sight of the Eiffel Tower lit up by lights in the distance. Several people groaned as they tried to settle their stomachs from the trip.

It was eerily quiet now that the humans didn't inhabit France and as we followed Victor through the empty streets towards the battleground, I shivered. Straightening my back, I focused on my anger and ignored the chill of fear creeping up my spine.

Achilles slipped his fingers through mine and moaned when just the touch brought his powers. His wings popped out of his back, almost hitting Ares.

"Watch it," Ares growled.

Achilles whispered, "I didn't mean to do that."

I rubbed his hand with my thumb and said, "Sorry."

He shook his head and kissed my cheek. "You have nothing to be sorry for. That has never happened before so I wasn't prepared."

Victor gave us a scalding look so we stopped talking.

We walked for what felt like hours before finally coming to a field of burned wood and ash that used to be a lush forest. Several of the halfbreeds, including Ares and I, growled at the ruined forest. Thousands of trees had been destroyed in the obviously man-made fire. Whatever their reason had been for destroying the forest, it just added to the anger and the need to tear something apart in all of us, the Sidhe who value nature included.

The presence of evil pressed down upon me as we walked farther into the opening and then we saw the vampire army. A familiar figure stood at the front with hybrid vampires beside him. I swallowed nervously as I thought about the possibility of having to fight my brother. I pulled my bow over my head and nocked an arrow.

Apollo stepped forward and spoke in a commanding voice, "You are acting in treason against the King of the World, Maurice. Drop your weapons or we shall be forced to attack you."

Zeus turned to Ares, Achilles, and I and waved us forward. "You're the leaders."

Ares and Achilles shrugged and Ares asked, "You want to respond?"

I smiled. "Sure." I walked out past our group and let my wings fully extend and my body glow brighter. "There is no king of the world, only an old vampire overstepping his place and committing extreme crimes, including murder, treason and torture. We are all equals. Unless you drop your weapons and allow us to pass so that we can kill Maurice for his crimes, we will be forced to fight you."

Apollo's shocked face was priceless. He took a moment to compose himself and then he said, "You will not see reason. I have no other choice but to punish you."

The vampires and dhampirs all hissed at us and licked their lips in excitement. I aimed my bow and released the arrow. Apollo jumped to the left, narrowly escaping the arrow, and it passed through the four vampires behind him, making them burst into ash at the touch of the sunlight on the tip of the arrow.

"Then let us fight!" I yelled.

Our army surged forward and the vampires and dhampirs ran to meet us. The screams of rage and pain covered everything else. Achilles, Ares, Koda, and Theseus took protective positions around me, preventing any from coming too close to me. I shot three more arrows, which killed an additional twelve vampires and two dhampirs. Vampires and dhampirs died all around me, while very few of our group fell, a good sign so far.

Ares and Koda fought side by side in half-shifts, cutting down our enemies with a speed that I only hoped to attain with practice. Achilles' sword flashed, quick as lightning, as he attacked, his focus never wavering from the battle.

Despite all of the vampires and dhampirs the men around me killed, the enemy continued to crowd closer, pushing the men even closer to me and preventing me from fighting. The battle finally grew too close so I hung my bow over my shoulder, placed my fists together and then separated them, forming my sword of light.

I held the sword in readiness, but Ares and the others were still keeping the vampires and dhampirs a safe distance away from me. In this moment, I watched the skill of Achilles' blade and the swiftness of Ares' movements with awe. The vampires pressed closer and forced the men to move even closer to me. "Stop protecting me and let me fight!" I yelled over the sounds of the battle.

Ares growled, but after killing two more vampires he stepped forward to break the circle around me. A vampire charged in and I brought my sword up, slicing him cleanly in half. My blood pumped harder and my body quivered in excitement as I started fighting. The men moved out a little farther, opening their circle and killing faster as they plowed deeper into the advancing enemy. My wings retracted due to the now limited space, but my body continued to glow as I fought with everything that I had. Bodies piled up around us and I realized that the vampires weren't just fighting, but fighting their way towards me. That realization didn't frighten me like it would have years before. Instead, it made me smile and renewed the vigor with which I fought.

We had to move deeper into the swarming masses due to the immense amount of dead bodies around us, which were making it impossible to walk. Achilles stayed beside me while Ares, Koda and Theseus were separated from us by the crowding enemy. I reined in my power to keep my reserves up and laughed joyously as I killed again and again. When I thought I was human, I never would have enjoyed killing. Now I knew what I was made for. I was made to end the evil in the world and right the balance. Dhampirs backed away from me when they got too close and I followed after them, cutting off whatever was closest to me and finishing off the being as it screamed.

I turned to find Achilles and Apollo battling each other, but surprisingly Apollo was holding his own against Achilles.

I turned around in time to decapitate a dhapmir running at me. I battled with vampires while trying to watch the fight between Achilles and Apollo at the same time. A vampire grabbed my sword hand and twisted, trying to break my wrist, which only pissed me off. Sunlight began seeping out of my pores and the vampire burst into flames and then turned to ash, drifting along the wind.

Achilles gasped in pain. I spun around and stared in shock as a blade was shoved through his chest and its bloody end dripped out the back. I moved towards him, but it was too late. I was always too late. Too slow.

"No!" I screamed as Achilles' light faded and then my own body dropped to the ground. Darkness surrounded me and cold spread through my limbs. The last thing I heard was Ares scream my name as I died beside Achilles.

TWENTY-TWO

ARES

My soul split in two, sapping half of my strength and making me stumble forward. Koda's heartrending howl confirmed what I knew had happened before I turned. I spun around and screamed Artemis' name, but it was too late.

Terror and dismay washed over me as my beautiful mate dropped to the ground beside Achilles and both of their lights faded.

I ripped through everyone and everything blocking my path to her. Vampires and dhampirs fled in terror and Sidhe and halfbreeds dove out of my way as I ran to her.

Koda made it to her body first and kept the vampires at bay, snarling and slashing at them in his half-shift. I dropped to the ground and picked her limp body up into my arms. Her head lolled to the left and her arms hung limply by her sides instead of wrapping around me as they should have. I howled in pain and cradled her against my chest as tears streamed down my face. My body reverted back to man and my throat changed with it.

"NO!" I screamed as the loss of her presence began to

resonate within my body. "Please Artemis, wake up," I whispered as I stroked her hair.

Not a single sound came from her. Her beautiful voice was gone. She was gone. I screamed and heard the keening sound I was making, which I knew sounded pathetic, but I didn't care. My mate was gone. I had nothing now.

The sounds of fighting ceased and Hera and Zeus dropped to their knees on the ground beside Achilles' body. Hera placed her hand against Achilles' face and screamed her despair.

Zeus looked from Artemis to Achilles with tears in his eyes, but made no sounds of loss. He stood up and said, "This battle is over for today."

Artemis' body was beginning to lose its warmth. I rubbed her arms to try to warm her and cradled her head against my shoulder, but she remained cold. Koda shifted to his wolf form and howled in grief. She was the love of my life, magical influence or not, I loved her more than anything else in the world. She was the greatest gift I'd ever been given and now she was gone.

I couldn't lose her! She had just come back into my life. I'd waited one hundred years to find her again and we'd only just been reunited. This couldn't be happening. I wouldn't let this happen!

"Hades!" I yelled as loud as I could. "Hades!"

A Sidhe as dark as night itself walked through the crowd and dropped to his knees in front of me. "I am here, Ares," he said in a voice as deep as the night was dark.

"Send me," I whispered.

The crowd which had been murmuring quietly a moment before, instantly went silent.

"Ares, I don't think..." Hades began softly.

I growled at him and stared into his eyes. "Send me!" I yelled.

"We can't do it here. We need to wait until we're somewhere safe so that we can protect your body as well as Artemis' and Achilles'," said Zeus from beside me.

Koda wrapped his furred body around me in an attempt to comfort me and I pushed him away. Comfort meant there was something to be sad about. I couldn't be sad about this because that meant that she was dead and I couldn't get her back. I would get her back. "I won't let her die. I promised her that I wouldn't let anything separate us, not even death. I have to go!"

"I understand. Hades will send you once her body is protected," Zeus said. I nodded in understanding and then he started to reach down towards Artemis.

I growled at him and spun up and around to protect her body from his touch. "Mine!" I yelled angrily. I held her body against mine, wishing my warmth would bring her back. Wishing this was just a dream.

Zeus raised his hands in the air. "I'm sorry," he said sadly, "Come, let's leave this place."

Hera picked Achilles up in her arms and let her wings out. She flew up above everyone's heads and wailed as she cradled her dead heir against her bosom, just as she'd done over one thousand years ago, when he had been born.

Zeus waited until Victor was beside me and then took to the skies after his wife.

"Let's go, Ares," Victor said quietly. "We need to hurry before the vampires change their minds and come back."

"Let them come. I will tear their hearts from their chests and feed it to them," I said as I started walking.

The sound of someone softly sobbing a few feet away

made me turn. Apollo sat on the ground staring at nothing. "I didn't know. I didn't know," he repeated over and over again.

"Didn't know what?" Victor asked angrily.

"I didn't know she was bound to him. If I had known...I wouldn't have told them to...I never wanted her to die. I just wanted to scare her and make her stay off the battlefield. I didn't know who he was to her," Apollo whispered as tears flowed down his face.

Koda snarled and lunged at Apollo who made no move to protect himself. I stepped into Koda's path and said, "Bring him with us. Alive."

Victor grabbed the halfbreed by the back of the neck and forced him to walk in front of us. The crowds parted as we walked and I growled at anyone who came too close. She wasn't going to be dead for long. I had to save her. I had to save her or give my life trying.

We'd known about this prophecy and yet it had been forgotten in the hectic life that we led. I might have been able to save her had I remembered it and consulted the other Sidhe. I might have kept her from dying if I'd only forced her to stay at Hera's Court. How could I have forgotten the prophecy?

Anger stirred within me, and I wanted to break something or someone. She had been taken from me again! I was supposed to be one of the most powerful beings on Earth. Only two generations from the original beings and yet I could not protect her. When the wolves had kidnapped her for the Vampire Queen, I'd wanted to tear down every building in search of her. Then Hera had stolen her and blocked her memories. Of all the times I'd wanted to kill that woman then had been the only time I might have actually done it. And now

Artemis was actually dead. Her cold, lifeless body lay in my arms as evidence.

Every part of me ached, and I shook in misery as her loss and distance became more evident. If I couldn't get her back, I would never see her smile again. I would never hear her laugh. Never see her blush. I'd never run with her in the forest.

She was my world. Nothing else mattered, but having her beside me. Not the fate of the world, not even the fate of my pack. How could I possibly continue to live without her hand in mine?

Dmitri led the way, claiming to know a place that was safe for us as well as him and not visited by other vampires. We walked for two hours before finally stopping at a lone building in the middle of a flower field. It was an old cathedral that had somehow survived the uprising of the preternatural world. Surprisingly even the stained-glass windows were still intact. I looked up to see the gargoyles staring out across the field as though to ignore our presence. The saints carved around the entrance glared accusingly, but I ignored their prejudice. Zeus pushed open the doors, which groaned at him for disturbing their peace.

"Koda check inside," I said as I adjusted my hold on Artemis' body.

Koda walked into the cathedral and came out a moment later, sneezing. *Only rats and dust in there.*

We walked into the cathedral, and I stopped a moment to admire the building. The stained-glass windows cast multi-colored shadows upon the wooden pews. A wide red carpet led to the front of the cathedral where a skeleton sat in a chair. Judging by his robes he must have been the priest.

Victor leaned over a basin of water which stood at the

entrance and whispered, "I've always wondered if this worked on us or not. Father told us that it didn't, but none have been willing to test the theory in front of me before." He put his hand into the water and splashed some onto his face. He frowned a moment and then smiled. "Guess not."

Dmitri led us through a side door which opened to a hallway where saints carved into the stone watched our passing with great sadness. I wanted to yell at them and tell them her death was not permanent, but remembered they were only stone carvings and did not understand our situation.

We rounded a corner and started down a narrow set of stairs which led underground to the catacombs I'd heard about long ago, but never visited.

Zeus' body glowed as we descended into the darkness, giving us enough light to see. Koda snapped up a rat which squeaked its disapproval of our presence.

I looked at Koda and asked, "What are you doing?"

I'm hungry. He said just as his stomach growled.

"That's disgusting, Koda. You don't know where that things been," Victor said as he kicked another rat out of his way.

The ground was dirt, but it was packed down so tightly that it resembled stone. Despite the exquisite cathedral above us, there was no architecture in the catacombs to speak of save the wooden skeletal structure that kept the earth from caving in on itself.

We weaved our way through the catacombs, following behind Dmitri, who stopped at a tomb with an x marked over it.

Dmitri broke the door open and walked inside. "X marks the spot," Apollo said softly.

Despite the circumstances a soft chuckle slipped past my lips, as well as Victor's. Victor nudged Apollo forward into the tomb and we filed inside.

Dmitri sat beside a stone sarcophagus with an image of a young woman carved into its lid. He rested his hand on top of one of her carved ones and whispered softly in French.

"Who's that?" I asked Victor softly.

"His wife. He was turned while he was still with her and he could not control the bloodlust when he went back to visit her."

"Is that why this cathedral hasn't been destroyed?" I asked.

Victor nodded. "My father agreed to leave this building intact at Dmitri's request."

A second sarcophagus sat beside Dmitri's wife, but its lid was blank. "Who is that?" I asked as I motioned towards it.

"No one lies there. That was supposed to be Dmitri's burial place when he died."

I walked to it and laid Artemis' body along its cold stone lid. Dmitri was still whispering quietly beside his wife's sarcophagus and I felt immense pity for him and a determination not to be in the same situation. I arranged Artemis' body comfortably and placed her hands on her stomach. She looked like an angel.

Hera was elsewhere in the catacombs, wailing through the wall of the tomb, her power beating against the stone walls. I knew I should be mourning the loss of my brother, but I couldn't think of his death while I held Artemis' lifeless hand in mine.

I walked with Victor and helped him secure the front door so that any passersby wouldn't walk in.

"Ares, think about it before you do anything rash," Victor pleaded with me as he followed me back into the room.

"I've thought about it enough. I'm going to get her and bring her back," I answered.

"Let us discuss it first. Seek council from Koda and your father. Please," Victor said with such concern in his voice that it made me stop to look at the vampire.

We'd known each other one thousand years and he'd never spoken to me with such evident worry. "Very well," I answered quietly. I turned to Koda who had been listening passively. "Koda?"

Koda turned his head, breaking the silent stare he'd had on Artemis' body. *Huh?*

"Do I go after Artemis or stay here and let her rot?" I asked.

Victor groaned and threw his hands up into the air. "You're impossible! Koda, does he go, possibly to his death, to *try* and possibly fail to get Artemis? Or does he stay here safe, happy and alive?"

Koda looked at Artemis' still body and then met my eyes. *Bring her back.*

Koda was the most emotional of my brothers' and the lack of emotion in his eyes frightened me. It could only mean one thing; he was bottling it up. That could result in a catastrophic event if he didn't release soon, especially since he was staying in wolf form. I debated whether to force him out of wolf form, but Zeus walked into the room, interrupting my thoughts.

"Finally, someone who thinks logically. Please, talk some sense into your son," Victor begged.

Zeus ignored all of us and walked to Artemis' side. He dropped to his knees and cradled her small hand between his two giant ones. "I am so sorry, child. We should have been there to save you. I should have been fighting beside my son. I have failed you." Silent tears slid down his face as he kissed the back of her hand. "I will never forgive myself for this."

Victor sighed softly. "So much for logical."

"Father," I whispered.

Zeus placed Artemis' hand on her stomach and walked to us. "Yes?"

"Do you think I should venture to Death's realm to try to barter for Artemis' soul? Or let her death be?"

Zeus shook his head. "I will have no part in this. I've lost one son and one daughter. I will not help you decide and possibly cause your death as well."

"Tell him not to go," Victor pleaded. "Tell him to stay."

Zeus shook his head again. "No, it is his decision. If he goes than he does so with my blessing. If he stays than he does so with my blessing. I am neutral and will remain neutral."

"Thank you, Father."

Zeus gripped my shoulder in a sign of affection and left the room.

"I'm going, Victor. I must. And I need to go now, before her body fully dies and Death permanently holds her."

Victor hissed and turned towards the door. "Well I'm not going to sit by and watch you die."

"Thank you, Victor."

He met my eyes and shook his head. "I hope you get her back. I do not wish to bury your body."

"I love you, too, man," I said in a silly tone, reminiscent of the human's stereotypical hippie voice to try to lighten his mood.

Victor shook his head and left the room.

Hades had followed us in and now stood silently beside me. I could sense he did not want to do what I was asking, but I also knew that he would do it if I asked.

"Send me. I have to get her back," I whispered without taking my eyes from Artemis' face.

"You know you might not be able to get her back. If Death decides to keep you there, too, I cannot return you to your body either. You may both die this night," said Hades in warning.

"I have no reason to return to my body if I can't bring her back," I answered. I kissed her lips and whispered, "I'm coming, Sunshine. I'm coming to bring you back from the darkness."

I lay down on the ground beside her and closed my eyes. "You're in charge," I told Koda who only huffed in response. I should have tried to console him since he was my only living pack mate at the moment, but I didn't want my focus to waver from Artemis.

Hades put his hands on my head and chest and spoke quickly in Latin. Pain surged through my body, but it was nothing compared to the pain I felt losing her. This pain I could handle. This was only physical pain. Darkness rolled over me, through me and then surrounded me.

Nothing moved. Nothing breathed. Nothing was anywhere. Anger overcame me and I growled and closed my eyes, focusing on my senses and searching for any movement. Any sound. Any smell.

"Death!" I yelled into the void.

I still couldn't sense anything and my wolf side did not like that fact. It was too close to being in a cage or being trapped for me. I inhaled and yelled, "Death! Show yourself!"

The darkness stirred and a hooded figure stepped out in front of me. Its cloak looked like it was formed from the darkness that surrounded us and made me wonder if it could consume a person if placed over them. The scythe it carried was at least seven feet long, a full foot taller than Death and had a wicked sharp edge that gleamed even in the darkness.

It raised its hand and instead of the black void where I had been, I now stood in a royal chamber and Death sat upon the throne. The carpet and upholstery were black instead of red like most kings would have. I supposed that black was a fitting color for Death's throne room, though I personally would have gone for a less cliché color myself, probably blue. Or purple, like Artemis' eyes.

Death stroked the scythe, which was now sitting beside it like a king would stroke his scepter. "Ares Lupine," it said in a voice like rocks grinding against each other, "I have longed to see your face in my realm."

"I regret to inform you that I am not yet dead."

Death laughed and said, "I am aware of that, Ares. I am also aware of the fact that you are here for two of the souls I received during your battle." It was odd not to see a face while talking to someone, but then again, Death wasn't really a person.

"I will take Achilles' soul back with me if you permit, but if you only allow me one soul than I will take my mate back. It is not her time. She still has a prophecy to fulfill." I walked closer to Death, wondering what game I was going to have to play to get Artemis back or what price might be asked of me.

Death stood and motioned for me to follow. It walked down a hallway lined with what looked like black velvet and with sconces made of bones. Pictures of beings in various states of torture hung every ten feet along the wall on the right side while paintings of battlefields pooling with blood lined the left side. I knew this was all just a conjured image, but it was going a long way to keep up the charade for me. Was there some point it was trying to make?

The sounds of moaning and wails began to echo down the hallway. The hair on the nape of my neck stood up and the wolf within me grew uneasy. Was this a trap? Or perhaps it was going to test me somehow?

The hallway ended at a large metal door, and Death pushed it open. The wailing grew incredibly loud as I stepped through the door to stand on a stone balcony overlooking a black river. Glittering silver specters swirled around inside the river and I realized that's where the moaning was coming from. "The river Styx?"

Death nodded. "Some of the beliefs of each religion are true. It is unfortunate the humans could not come together to understand the complete truths of each."

A young girl, no older than seven years old, walked across the bank on the opposite side of the river towards the water. Her eyes were lost and full of fear as she stepped into the water, but as soon as it closed over her head her fear evaporated and a smile spread over her face.

I stared at the writhing black water a moment longer before asking. "Why did you bring me here?"

"There are some who would die to see this," Death quipped.

Death was trying to joke with me. At another time I might have laughed, but there was no humor in my heart at the moment. "Are you going to make me swim through it to find my mate's soul?" I asked.

Death laughed. "You would not survive the waters. The others would eat you alive if the water did not take you first. No, Ares Lupine, I have brought you here to see the truth of fate. There is no heaven or hell. Your soul simply glides around the waters until I release it to disappear and let you rest."

That was partially reassuring since I'd always assumed I was going to Hell for all of the beings I'd killed, but also slightly disheartening to know we simply vanished.

Death walked back to the first room and sat on the throne. "Why have you come to me?"

"You know the answer to that question," I growled.

"Yes," Death said with amusement in its voice, "But apparently, *you* do not."

It waved a hand and Artemis appeared in human form beside Death. A light pulsed where her heart was, her soul, but a second light pulsed in her stomach as well.

"I'm surprised that you would so easily give up the soul of your unborn child," Death said mockingly.

I gaped at the small pulsing light in my mate's stomach as Death's words sunk in. Artemis was pregnant. That's why she had thrown up. I'd thought it had been nerves, but obviously, it was more than that.

"What price would you pay for your mate and your child's souls?" asked Death as it ran a hand along Artemis' side.

I did *not* like it caressing my mate in such a manner. I tried to rein in my anger so as not to upset it. I couldn't afford to piss it off and lose my mate and my child. How could I have been such a fool? How could I have let this go unnoticed? "I have given you thousands of souls and I will give you thousands more for their lives. Give my mate and my child back to me!" I commanded, losing control at the sight of it continuing to touch Artemis.

"Only gods may command me, Ares of the Werewolves," Death answered slowly. The taste of its fear tickled my tongue and excited the wolf within me. How long had it been since Death had been afraid? I wasn't naive enough to assume I was the first to frighten it, but I was angry enough to want to be the last to. It grabbed its scythe, standing up and blocking my view of Artemis.

My body began glowing as my anger grew and my Sidhe powers released. I moved faster than a human eye could track, stopping inches from Death. I had no fear of this thing and I had no fear of death. It had angered me, and I was tired of its games. I yelled, "I am the God of War! Give them to me!"

CONNECT WITH CATHERINE BANKS

I really appreciate you reading my book! I hope you enjoyed it.

Please consider leaving a review at your favorite site.

Here are some ways to connect with me:

www.catherinebanks.com

Follow me on BookBub: https://www.bookbub.com/authors/catherine-banks

Join my Patreon: http://www.patreon.com/catherinebanks

Purchase items handmade by Catherine: http://Etsy.com/shop/TurboKittenInd

ABOUT THE AUTHOR

Catherine Banks is a USA Today bestselling fantasy author who writes in several fantasy subgenres and has multiple pseudonyms. She began writing fiction at only four years old and finished her first full-length novel at the age of fifteen. She is married to her soulmate and best friend, Avery, who she has two amazing children with. After her full-time job, she reads books, plays video games, and watches anime shows and movies with her family to relax. Although she has lived in Northern California her entire life, she dreams of traveling around the world. Catherine is also C.E.O. of Turbo Kitten Industries™, a company with many hats including being a book publisher and Etsy store full of nerdy fun.

facebook.com/catherinebanksauthor
twitter.com/catherineebanks
amazon.com/author/catherinebanks
bookbub.com/authors/catherine-banks

MORE FROM CATHERINE BANKS

ADULT PARANORMAL & FANTASY ROMANCE SERIES

Zodiac Shifters Paranormal Romance Series

Centaur's Prize

Tiger Tears

Lion About

Ciara Steele Novella Series

True Faces

Barbaric Tendencies

ADULT REVERSE HAREM PARANORMAL & FANTASY ROMANCE SERIES

Her Royal Harem Series

Royally Entangled

Royally Exposed

Royally Elected

Royally Enraged

Her Royal Harem, The Complete Series

The Demon's Fair

Her Royal Harem, The Coloring Book

Wings of Vengeance Series

Of Dragons and Cruelty

Of Minotaurs and Sacrifice

Wings of Vengeance, The Complete Series

Anderelle: Minloa Trilogy

Queen of the Stars

Empress of the Galaxy

Goddess of the Universe

Anderelle: Minloa, The Complete Series

Bonds of Madness Series
Sealing the Deal
Racing the Clock

Her Super Harem Series
Lucky Strike

Her Hellish Harem Duet
A Demon's Heart
A Demon's Soul*

*Coming Soon

MORE FROM CATHERINE BANKS

<u>**STANDALONE YOUNG ADULT PARANORMAL & FANTASY ROMANCE BOOKS**</u>

Monster Academy

Daughter of Lions

Lady Serra and the Draconian

Of Sky and Sea

The Last Werewolf

Sybil Deceived

<u>**STANDALONE YOUNG ADULT PARANORMAL & FANTASY REVERSE HAREM ROMANCE BOOKS**</u>

Moon Academy

<u>**STANDALONE ADULT PARANORMAL & FANTASY ROMANCE BOOKS**</u>

Demonic Contract

Anja's Secret

Dragon's Blood

Last Ama Princess

Transforming Rose
Alys of Asgard
Phoenix Possessed
Stone Heart

STANDALONE URBAN FANTASY BOOKS
The Pawn

CHILDREN'S BOOKS
Calvin's Alien Adventure

MORE FROM DAISY EMORY

The Boyfriend Deal

Their Purple Girl

ACCIDENTAL MOBSTER SERIES
Accidental Mobster
Unintentional Pirate
Suddenly Baroness*

*Coming Soon

9 781946 301598